www.11-9.co.uk

Occasional demons

Raymond Soltysek

First published by

303a The Pentagon Centre
36 Washington Street
GLASGOW
G3 8AZ
Tel: 0141-204-1109
Fax: 0141-221-5363
E-mail: info@nwp.sol.co.uk
http://www.11-9.co.uk

A catalogue record for this book is available from the British Library.

11:9 is funded by the Scottish Arts Council National Lottery Fund.

ISBN 1-903238-12-9

Typeset in Utopia
Designed by Mark Blackadder

Printed by WS Bookwell, Finland

The following terms are Trademarks and are recognized by the publishers as such:
Vienetta
Sunblest
Yale
Timex
CKone
Wranglers

The publishers would like to thank the Royal Bank of Scotland plc for permission to use their logo.

Contents

The practicality of magnolia

By the time Isobel discovered that the boy sleeping in her upstairs bedroom was wanted for attempted murder, it was too late to turn back. And anyway, he was co-operative and quiet and, provided he didn't realize that she knew, he'd no reason to turn against her.

She'd suspected something even as she'd watched him come down the road from the west. The road led past a couple of holiday homes, a few caravans, the cottages of the Fitzgibbons and old Sandy Macdonald, and ended at the automated lighthouse. It had puzzled her that anyone wearing shabby training shoes and a hooded sweatshirt should come from that direction late on a late summer Wednesday looking for bed and breakfast for a few days, for there was nowhere to come from.

'Could Ah have a bath?' he'd asked, edgy, his head turned down. 'Ah huvny had a good wash furra wee while – been on the road, like. Ah widnae want to dirty yir clean sheets.'

'Of course,' she'd said. 'When you've finished, put your clothes in the laundry basket in the bathroom and I'll wash them. You're very welcome to join me for supper if you like. Just toast and butter.'

'Aye, that'd be great. Ta.'

He had eaten hungrily but civilly, and asked if she had a newspaper, but she said she never bought them because they were filled with terrible happenings, and he'd smiled and nodded and agreed. She had to apologise too for not having a television – she found them noisy, she said, and after James died, well ... but the boy hadn't seemed too bored listening to Radio 4 with her, and he had gone to bed early without asking about public houses nearby, not that there was one.

She'd slept badly that first night, though not because of the boy, since she felt safe enough with her door bolted and the telephone moved beside her bed; besides, no-one had responded to her 'Vacancies' sign all summer, so she certainly couldn't be choosy. She'd listened to the unfamiliar creaks of the floorboards, imagined the regularity of his breathing, thought she heard him cry out, once, around three. When light had come up, when the magpies had begun to swirl around the eaves, encouraging their last shrieking chick to fly, she'd still been awake.

'When can Ah come back the night?' he'd asked after breakfast. He'd sounded childish, reluctant to raise the question at all, looking for an 'Och don't bother,' from her. Not that she had children herself, but she'd trained as a primary school teacher before marrying James. Knew their ways.

'You don't have to stay away if you don't want to,' she'd said. 'Go for a walk, over the hill, if you feel like it. There's some nice lochans up there, and you get a lovely view of the bay from the top. Just come back whenever you need to.'

He seemed grateful, went up the hill and returned in the afternoon. 'It's great up there,' he said, flushed, and told her about bullets he'd found, hundreds and hundreds of them. From the war, she said, the whole area was evacuated, used as practice for D-Day. The bullets were quite safe, though. He'd hung out her washing, made his bed, hoovered upstairs, then sat at the bottom of the garden with a pot of tea. She'd watched him fall asleep in the sunlight, the shadows of beech leaves flickering over his face. Almost hairless, sunken sockets dark. His chin fell onto his scrawny chest.

'Eh, see yir grass. Ah'll cut it for ye,' he offered when she brought him sandwiches – no extra, because he'd been so helpful, she said. 'Ah'd like tae stay, furra cuppla weeks mibbe. Ah huvnae much money but. Thought mibbe Ah could dae a few jobs. Pay ma way, like.'

She made her mind up then, seeing the possibilities in an instant. 'I do have something that needs done,' she said, and took him to the garage, behind James' Volvo where she'd neatly stacked the tins.

'I'd like the rooms painted,' she said. 'It's been years since they were done. We had decorators in. My husband liked magnolia, you see. Because it goes with anything.'

'Right,' he said. 'A wee freshen up?'

'Well, a bit more than that,' and she pulled the cans of paint out one by one. 'I got these delivered. Awfully difficult to get up here.'

He weighed them in his hands, brushing dust from lids. Coral Blush. Dusty Jade. Sienna and Golden Amber. Gloss and satin and colourwash. Tins and tins of Brilliant White, Diamond White, Sparkling White. And then rollers and brushes and brand new stepladders, gleaming steel.

He pulled a face at the Mulberry Crush emulsion. 'Is it no a bit much?'

'It is a bit daft, I suppose. All these colours. The local man who does the painting and decorating would think I was gone in the head. Eccentric old Sassenach, he'd say, and I've been here forty years.' He was shaking his head. 'I wonder if you would do it? Just as much as you can while you're here.'

It would take weeks, he said, but he had nowhere to go, so if she wouldn't mind him staying ... no, she wouldn't, and he'd have all his meals there and he needn't pay for his bed though she couldn't promise to pay him any more. That was fine by him, very generous of her. His hand seemed as frail and thin as hers when they shook on the deal.

He started on the morning she found out, driving in the Volvo to Acheracle for extra bread and tea and vegetables, listening to the radio station broadcasting from Glasgow. A girl, *lying gravely ill in hospital,* battered, police searching for her boyfriend, *Charles McCausley, twenty-one,* a perfect description, even of his clothes.

May be desperate.

Do not approach.

'A lodger, you say, Mrs McCandlish?'

'Yes, Mrs Farmer. An American girl. Walking round Scotland. Very brave of her, if you ask me.'

'Foolish I'd say. You hear terrible things with these serial killers on the loose everywhere. Is she staying long?'

'She might. But she's very quiet. I don't think you'll be seeing much of her around here,' and she packed the car quickly to be off home.

The ceiling gleamed white. Snow White. He'd masked along the cornicing, the edge crisp and neat against the dullness of the old magnolia, and he was sitting at the table drinking tea. 'Just while it dries a bit, like,' he said, flinching as she pushed her way past the hallstand, the telephone table and the old blanket box he'd moved into the kitchen.

'Of course', she said, 'don't be silly. You're allowed a rest you know,' and she cut him some fruit cake she made for visitors and watched the muscles in his neck uncoil. 'Take all the time you need.'

The next day, Isobel visited her sister-in-law in Tobermory. They spoke of James – what a good man he'd been – and Agnes' husband Archie, senile and hostile in an old folks' home run by an English couple – more incomers – and about the young American woman staying with Isobel. So very helpful. Then the Volvo wouldn't start, to catch the last boat back to Kilchoan.

She telephoned five times before he picked up the receiver.

'Hullo,' he said, his voice strange, as if on a starting block.

'Hello, it's Mrs McCandlish,' she replied, and wasn't surprised by the rush of relief she heard. 'I'm afraid I've missed the last boat. I won't be back until the morning. Can you manage on your own?'

'Aye. Ah'll just get on wi it. Is that all right?'

'Yes, fine.'

'Listen,' he said, 'just leave it till later. Ah'll have it done by the afternoon. It'll be a surprise tae see it finished.'

'Okay then,' she said, absurdly flattered.

She got home after five and stepped into a hallway that was orange, deep, burned, smoky orange, and the wood even darker, almost toffee. 'Ah had tae gie it two coats: it's a really deep colour,' and she gasped and gaped and felt she was wrapped in a warm blanket. 'It's wonderful,' she said, and his head came up, pleased and cocky.

'Huv Ah done a good job?'

'Just – wonderful.'

She found herself cooking real food again, shepherd's pie, and proposed he paint the bedroom next. She would sleep in the sitting room, and would he mind doing something a bit special for her? He'd first asked what, and sounded dubious when she showed him the heavy greaseproof paper and suggested stencils – 'It wullnae work,' he said three times – but she ferreted out a craft knife from James' old toolbox and showed him how.

He was sullen, put out for a day, but the work overtook his mood and he gave her a flower frieze only a whisper darker than the lavender of the walls. She set the room out just right, the cream lace bed-linen the best she had, the woodwork and furniture polished rich and sensuous. She read for a while in bed, her attention constantly drawn to the flowers and the walls, and when she slept she dreamed of a man for the first time ever, though when she woke she couldn't remember who he was or what he looked like.

She insisted he take two days off, but he showed no sign of going anywhere or doing anything, simply pacing up and down the beach before breakfast and sunbathing in the secluded back garden in the afternoon. He stripped off his t-shirt and she saw that he wasn't scrawny or frail, but taut and tightly corded across his shoulders and down his arms, and she wondered how often he held and how often he hit the girl. Once he did exercises, push-ups and sit-ups. She watched his muscles tense and slacken, the sweat glistening and pouring down his back, the tattoo of a dragon, blue and red and green, flex and stretch on his shoulder blade, and she felt ashamed, a stupid old woman.

The kitchen was next, sunshine yellow and cornflower blue, and when it was finished Isobel made lemon tea and a special meal for them, something foreign that astounded Mrs Farmer.

'Well, Mrs McCandlish, I've never known you to want capsicums before. Is it something fancy you're cooking for your young American friend?'

'Yes it is.' Isobel scanned the notices behind Mrs Farmer's head. A ceilidh at the Salen hall. Local watercolours by that strange Dutch woman. 'It's her birthday, you know.'

'Oh I see.' A face appeared behind the shopkeeper's. A photograph. 'It's quite a while she's staying, is it not?'

HAVE YOU SEEN THIS MAN?

'I suppose so.'

MAY BE HIDING ALONG WEST COAST.

'Still, that's good news for you. It's not often you get such a client even during the season. It's funny we never see her around though.'

STOLEN BOAT.

'Och, she's very quiet. She reads a lot,' and she took the whole twelve, red and orange and yellow and green, their skins waxy and breathtaking. At home she put them in a blue bowl in the centre of the kitchen table and thought they were better than flowers.

'Will you be wanting to leave soon?' she asked.

'Naw,' he said, then urgently, 'How, d'ye want me tae go?'

'No, no, you're doing an excellent job. I'm delighted. It's just – I thought you might have to be moving on.' She wanted to say it might be safer.

'Ah'm okay.' He scratched his forearm, red strips flaring under the tanned skin. 'Ah want tae finish the job.'

The upstairs bedroom became deep terracotta, the room which James had used as a study became mulberry, both ceilinged in dazzling white, one more outrageous than the other. She loved them both, she said. He painted the stairwell blue, the insides of cupboards white, the utility room at the back of the kitchen bright green. One by one he picked them off, and all that was left was the sitting room. They sat there, looking at the last of the magnolia walls, listening to a comedy quiz show which he said he was beginning to enjoy.

'Ah'll strip the paint aff the fireplace if ye like,' he said. 'Ye've goat the strippers in the garage, and some varnish. It'll take a few extra days mind.'

'Do you think it's worth it?'

'Aw aye. It'll look great. 'sides, might as well. Out wi the auld, in wi the new, eh?'

'Yes,' she said. 'We'll just clear the mantelpiece.'

She fetched a cardboard box from the cupboard under the stairs, began to pack the accumulated paraphernalia of a long life: photographs of their parents, James in Navy uniform, her on her wedding day, always looked like Deanna Durbin his uncle Angus said. He dusted each quickly as she passed it to him. Candlesticks. Two china dolls. A tiny silver-plated box. Her fingers shook and it slipped between them, smacking loudly off the hearth rail. The top flew open and something small and light flicked across the room under her chair.

'Ah'll get it,' he said.

'It's all right, I'll do it.' She brushed past him and was on her knees, her hand exploring the tight space beneath the chair.

'Is it valuable? Looked like a pearl.'

'No, nothing like that.' She felt her fingertip scrape against it, and she stretched a little farther, dragging it towards her. 'It's nothing, just an old reminder of James.' It disappeared into her apron pocket. 'I forgot I even had it.'

It took him the best part of a week, brushing on chemicals that blistered when they splashed onto his skin. Careless, he said, and she made him wash his hands in warm soapy water and gave him plasters and rubber gloves when he went back to work.

When the fireplace was finished, she did admit it was worth the effort, the wood deep and dark and lustrous. She ran her fingers over it.

'Yer photies'll look good up there now, eh?'

'They'll look tremendous. Thank you. For all you've done.'

'Aye well. Ah'm getting to stay here, amn't Ah? So it's nuthin.'

'Don't be silly. It's become very important to me. Until you started, I didn't realize how important it was.'

He shuffled, too embarrassed to comprehend an old woman's feelings. 'Ye don't say much about yer husband. Whit he was like and stuff.'

'Oh, he was a man. A bit like you I suppose.'

'Aye? Whit way?'

'Just some of the things he did.' She gathered up their tea cups to take them to the kitchen. 'Perhaps when you've done the sitting room we should make a start on the outside of the house. What about sugar pink?' she said, and they laughed at the image. He made a joke about her house being like the Forth Rail Bridge and how he would have to start all over again, and though she knew that wouldn't happen she said it was a good idea.

He took time over the last of the painting, not deliberately but perhaps subconsciously. Hardly surprising really. He left each coat of emulsion for a full day to dry, and then the same with the gloss, and he filled holes and cracks and sanded to get a perfect finish. She saw little of the room, the dust sheets and ladders making it difficult – even dangerous – to push through the door, but she had the sense of subaqueous-jade light mellowing and pouring out into the orange hall.

'How are you getting on?' she called. He'd been nervy, moving in a funny, jerky way all morning, so she guessed it was almost completed. 'Shall I put some tea on?'

'Naw, no yet. Ah'm nearly done. Mibbe another twenty minutes.'

Nearly done. Twenty minutes.

She quietly unplugged the telephone from the hall, took it to her bedroom and connected it to the socket by her bed. The policeman in Mallaig was very helpful, very polite, said it wasn't at all unusual that Isobel hadn't realized who her lodger was until now.

'You know', she said, 'I even told Mrs Farmer at the shop it was a girl staying with me. I thought it would sound scandalous. Whatever will she think now?'

The sergeant laughed. 'Don't you worry about that. Just try not to alarm him. We've a car out now that can be with you in about half an hour.'

She sat on the edge of the bed, gathering herself, trembling slightly with the power of what she'd done. She smoothed her hair, her apron, felt the sharp little bump in the pocket, and took out the tooth. A young woman's tooth.

What bother she'd had, searching the floor of the hotel room the morning after their wedding night, keeping it from James all these years hidden in the lining of the little silver box. She held it up to the light. It was perfect, no decay, no fillings, far too healthy, good roots. Her jaw had ached for weeks after he'd done it. She ran her fingernail over the enamel, pale, translucent.

Off-white.

She suspended it momentarily over the waste-paper basket, then dropped it in and took the telephone back to the hall table to wait.

The boy went meekly when the huge policemen

came for him. 'Don't worry', they said when they'd locked him in the car, 'he'll never find out it was you. The report will just say "An Informant".' Someone would be round later for a statement, and she'd been very brave. Isobel saw their eyes drawn beyond her shoulder to the colours within and noted the scratch of a head, a slight curl of the lip.

Not to everyone's taste.

Thank you, thank you very much for everything, she told them, and she closed the door softly but firmly on the men.

Teuchter dancing when the lights go out

My left hand switched off last night.

Something inside me broke the connection and the nerves went dead. Just like that, out like a light. One millisecond, electrical pulses course along neural pathways. The next, gone, cold, defunct, and the whole thing's ready for the scrap yard.

I had a glass in my hand at the time. It dropped, bouncing off the padded arm of the chair, sending the cat bee-lining under the sofa. Just as well it was a vodka, not a cup of coffee to scald my legs. Not that they would feel it. They switched off months ago.

Allison came in, asked me if I was all right. I said yeah, just clumsy. I didn't tell her, seemed no point. She wiped up the puddle. I said she looked tired – fucking platitude – and she said yes she was. She asked me if I needed anything, I said a body transplant, and she smiled and kissed me goodnight, her lips dry against my cheek. She tidied up in the kitchen, opening and closing cupboards a few times. The kettle was boiled for her hot chocolate, the cat's litter tray was shaken. Then she went to bed.

I sat there and studied the switched-off hand. It looked no different, knuckles bulging, wrinkles, fine hairs. The nails were bitten badly, a lifelong habit I'll finally break if I can't get my bloody fingers near my mouth. Every cloud, they say.

I turned it over with my right hand. Soft hands. No manual work and lousy at DIY. Pink fingerprints. Long life line. Very long life line. Bastard.

Left hands are useless things anyway. Can't write love letters with them, or bowl a yorker, or toss yourself off in the middle of the night reading a porno mag from your secret store. They fight against learning to juggle, sulk awkwardly when meeting somebody new. Fucking hopeless, they are.

This is how I do it, since the rage left. The part of me I lose, the part which switches off, is made redundant. Always was superfluous. Never really needed that bit, did I darling? The legs were fine: gawky extremities which wore out expensive shoes, and the left one (left ones again, note) was crap at football. The prick was a bit trickier, though. Its use had to be redefined. Now, it's a convenient bit of pipework to connect to the plastic bag that fills at my side during the day.

Wasn't always like that, of course. In the beginning, we gave our genitals nicknames, they spoke to each other in silly voices and then we'd laugh at our childishness. She always made me feel good. Sometimes wonderful.

Like that weekend, a crisp New Year when we said let's do something different, and we lorded it up at some laird's long-pawned castle. There were claymores on the wall of the banquet hall, and round shields with those wee peaks in the middle like seventeenth-century Gaultier bras, built for the big, big women of the north. Settees of every period, every style, floral, gold filigree, brown dralon. Mantle shelves piled with stuff, antique candlesticks beside plastic snowstorms of Buckingham Palace and a gold 1960s James Bond DB5 complete with working ejector seat and bullet-proof shield. Owning a stately home's easy, just never ever throw anything away, it's bound to become a collector's item. And I had two of those Aston Martins, and a fucking Batmobile.

The ceilidh band had an accordionist the women dropped dead for, and a drummer who wore a tartan nightshirt and had red hair half way down his back and a definite fancy for Allison. They pummelled their music out, and the wee violinist in the short black skirt whirled round and round and stamped her feet, and her thighs made all the men shudder and toast her with the whisky, flowing amber, warm, reddening noses and making belches peppery. As much was spilled between clinking glasses as was drunk, and the kisses were deep and aromatic.

The floor was ace, shining abalone, perfect for dancing. Oh fuck, the dancing. We were wild with it, charging up and down, in and out, under arms and over skipping feet, stripping the willow and dashing the white sergeant. The pounding of a stitch, breathlessly working it off again, the feel of a waist, spun round the inside of the forearm, lost, whirling off to another grip, replaced – tight, hard, slim waists, eager to be held, desperate to be released. Allison laughed, shone perfect-cheekboned, flirted maniacally and always found her way back to me, and we leaned our foreheads together and mingled sweat turning rapidly cold in the lank bits of hair we flicked from our eyes. We collapsed against each other, wheezed half way off the dance floor until the band struck up and one of us said *Oh yeah! I know how to do this* and turned to begin again and again. We'd be called into an eightsome, arms arcing us over, *join us, join us,* and off we'd go. And I couldn't help directing traffic, *I'm a teacher, veteran of social dancing,* I'd say, *Ah-heel, toe, heel, toe, one-two-three turn,* and Allison would laugh and do it wrong deliberately, *no, no, round THAT way,* and I'd realize the fun all lay in fucking it up, reeling about in a rabble of skirt and shoe and twisting heads.

'Til three we went on, and made lifelong friends we never saw again, and the drummer got the message and toasted us and slapped me on the back. We all held conversations like running battles along the mahogany corridors, snipers popping heads out of doorways to fire jokes at us.

We went to our room and made love like athletes, getting embarrassed in mid flow by the squeaking bed, Allison flipping the mattress onto the floor with one superhuman finger and covering me with kisses. Her legs were over my shoulders when I came the deepest ever in her, and I watched myself laugh in the wardrobe mirror and I proposed to her then and there, even though we'd already been married for three years. She snaked her thighs around my waist and accepted, and we lay for an hour and found the mattress five times as heavy when we put it back on the bed.

We left early in the morning, after top'n'tailing in a bath as big as a submarine pen, washing each other's toes and losing the soap just so I could look for it in the places that made her squeak. This is the best, we said, the best, and I don't think we were ever happier.

I heard Allison's bedroom door open, her footsteps slippered soft along the hallway. She stopped, perhaps on the point of coming in, her hand reaching out to the doorknob. Then she turned and went back. Let her sleep.

I've been told. Bit by bit I'll switch off. Left arm next, probably. Right hand, arm. Hearing. Sight. My bowels have been opened, and my tongue will be stopped.

But my brain won't. It'll reel on, disconnected from all the switched-off fragments. Nothing listening to it. Nothing obeying it.

I'm ready for it, though. I know all the steps. Gay Gordons. Strip the Willow. Canadian Barn Dance. Military Fucking Two Step.

I'll be teuchter dancing.

Afterbirth

The clearness of the air was almost tangible, like newly cleaned windows. Margaret could see all the way across the moor, to the trig point, west to the line of Forestry Commission land, east to the shepherd's house, whitewashed, tiny and snug like a scrap of polystyrene litter wedged in a grass bank. She had to shield her eyes when she looked upward, the first real sunshine of the year; occasionally, a bird whirred overhead, bulleting past.

The last time she'd been up here, it had been with Carlos and the boys. Seemed like years ago. Charlie had held their hands tightly, swinging between them, his little fat legs dangling. He'd pretended to be brave but she could see he was unsure of the vastness of the place, the brownness. He'd kicked a bird's skull into the ditch, then cried when Joe told him what it had once been. His older brother had laughed, and run off, hurdling tall grass, to chase McTavish who had gone off scavenging, and Margaret had cuddled Charlie and wiped away his tears.

To her right, a brace of pheasant shot up twenty feet in the air as if someone had up-and-undered them. They struggled for aerial stability then flustered off, fat and ungainly. McTavish up to his tricks again. Mad spaniel. He came slobbering out of the grass, tongue lolling impossibly long, eyes wild. He looked at her just once, then loped off along the track, looking for something more exciting. Sheep. Perhaps a deer, if he was lucky.

She wondered if the boys missed this. Maybe not: they were young, and a beach of hot sand and pedalos and traders who bartered and fussed over children would seem like heaven. And naughty little Joe was just at the age when he might appreciate the topless girls. Damn it, she missed them: and what did she have to offer? Shingle, rotting seaweed, cold breakers, the odd inscrutable grey blob three hundred yards out which peered at freezing humans in day-glo jackets. 'Look, there's a seal!' she would say and they would go 'where?' and lob pebbles when they got bored. Joe's first postcard said that his father had taken them to Aqua World. He had thrown a fish to a dolphin. It had waved a flipper at him. The front of the card showed a livid orange sunset, a couple walking hand in hand: 'España – Where Dreams Come True', it said. She'd kept it under her pillow, hoping it would stop her crying herself awake, but it hadn't.

They'd sounded so excited to begin with, tiny voices tinny on the end of the telephone line, talking about how they'd met their daddy's family who spoiled them with sweets and toys and adventures. Joe had even been taken to a bull fight, slippery blood gushing hot; she'd screamed down the phone, saying no, no, my boy shouldn't see this, this is wrong, and had slammed the telephone receiver against the wall when Carlos simply laughed. Then Walker the lawyer told her to stop being hysterical, she would upset 'delicate negotiations involving diplomatic channels'.

Male diplomats, no doubt.

She was sweltering and needed a drink, so she left the path, skipping over the ditch and cutting east towards the shepherd's house. McTavish came bolting behind her, careering past through her legs, almost toppling her. A grouse flushed, squawking at them, and the dog skelped off in its direction, making the tall grass thunder as he went. Their father had bought them a new dog. Of course. She could picture him, handsome, sexy in his t-shirt and jeans, arms filled with gangly puppy and largess. Jacqueline, her best friend, bridesmaid, couldn't understand why she had thrown him out, had called her a fool because she made do with Alasdair, red-haired, freckled, unashamedly missionary. 'What's he got that Carlos hasn't?' she asked. It wasn't what he had, it was what he didn't have.

A fist.

Stuck in her face. Threatening. Never more, but more than enough.

It was a straightforward twenty-minute hike to the

cottage, the ground dry but giving. She'd said hello to the shepherd at the last-but-one barn dance, when she jigged half the men in the town off their feet while Carlos fumed in the corner. She hung back from returning to their table as long as she could, then she finally summoned up the courage and he grabbed her wrist, hissed 'bitch, slut' in her ear until the taxi came. He'd leaned close, and the smell of him, the aftershave and sweat and lager, made her head swim. No-one said goodnight to her, though some waved to Carlos. A good man, was Carlos, accepted as far as an outsider could be. She'd never gone anywhere in public with him again.

The cottage was deserted: it was the lambing, so the shepherd would be busy on the hills or down at the farm. He wasn't really a shepherd, not the romantic type anyway, more a seasonal odd-job man. Work was scarce on the island. That's what Carlos had said, over the telephone from the airport four hours after he'd been due to bring the boys back from their weekend visit and she'd climbed the walls because his phone rang out and his flat was locked up when she'd gone to find out what the hell was going on. I'm going back for work, been offered a job, I'm taking the boys, well-spoken airport announcer in the background. Back? He left twenty years ago and their children couldn't speak the language, even though he insisted on Jose and Carlos for names, and they had no knowledge of their Spanish relatives other than a one-month visit from an aunt with olive skin and red lips and preposterous nails who had a husband called Manuel for Christ's sake. They had fallen in *amor* with the island, so green they said, the colours of the heather, and they made a mean sangria. Carlos had come home from the pub one evening, thrown his dinner against the wall, what's this muck he'd said, and his sister had shouted at him, smacked him across the ear for abusing his wife. He'd shut himself away in the sitting room all night, watching football on the telly with his brother-in-law. Men, she'd said, what *bastardos*.

Bring them back, she'd begged, let's discuss this. No, he'd said, he didn't have time, the flight was being called, and she'd shouted you can't do this, as the tannoy pinged and the line went dead.

The rear of the cottage was shaded and chilly. In contrast to the well-kept frontage, the back garden was spattered with junk: a scooter with no engine, a tractor's steering wheel, a blanket spread on what was probably the lawn, one corner turned underneath. A line of shirts and vests and underpants, all the same dirty cream colour, hung out to dry. McTavish snuffled around, scenting collies, always good for a laugh, a rough and tumble. She wondered at the psychology of a man with no family, no connections, no responsibilities, no neighbours, who kept the front of his house tidy and left the back to moulder. Strange folk.

Backed up against the wall was a huge sink, three-inch thick brown stone. It had been propped up on bricks, but these had collapsed, making one end of the sink drop: a dripping standpipe formed a wedge of water. Margaret slipped off her jacket and slung it over the dry lip of the sink. She twisted the green, furry tap and water ran, sputtering. It was ice cold, straight from the hills. She sluiced it over her head, gasping, and gulped some from her cupped hands. It tasted sweet.

She peered over the edge into the water at the other end of the sink. She saw her own reflection for a second, and then the dark, dark liquid threaded green with silken algae. It floated delicately, moving in the current of things, things breast-stroking the depths, dark things in the dark, solid depth. What things?

Frogs.

Fat with spawn.

She jumped back. Silly, but she'd never liked frogs. Their coldness, their fragility, the thinness of their skins frightened her. Carlos made Joe laugh once, telling boyhood stories of how he exploded frogs with a straw up their bottoms. The thought of it had made her feel sick. She had once scandalized Joe by swerving to avoid a frog slap-slapping its way across the road. Why'd you do that, Mum, you don't like frogs, he'd said, and she'd told him that that didn't mean she wanted to squash them. Boys. Always wanting to hurt. She wondered if they ever grew up.

The path from the cottage was worn away to rust-red soil by feet and sheep and the occasional Land Rover. It was time to be getting back: the children usually telephoned around tea time, and she wanted to hear them, confirm her suspicions. Half a year they'd been away. When are you coming over? they asked. I miss you Mummy, big Joe, cool at seven but admitting that. And Charlie. He said little now, merely listened to her voice in awed silence and then cried softly about accidents during the night.

She wondered what they made of it all. They weren't old enough to understand the finality of 'it's finished', and to want to come home would betray their father. The solution was easy. Come over. Be together. We want you and Daddy ... a new life here, Daddy promised. A new start. Try again, what do you say?

The path curved around a clump of trees, and a small figure approached her, a reprobate of a collie at its heels. The shepherd. He was stooped, making him seem even smaller than his wiry five-foot three. She imagined his beard was greasy and smelled of pipe tobacco, but he was one of the island's quiet gentlemen, prone only to sporadic outbursts of violence, usually over drink. He waved jerkily.

'Mrs Criado. How are you today?' he said, as if it hadn't been months since they'd last met.

'I'm fine, Sandy, thanks.'

'Are you up here on your own?'

'No. McTavish is with me.' She looked around. 'Come to think of it, he's disappeared. I'm surprised he's not attacking your dog.'

'Och, Jake's not up to playing any more. Are you, boy?' He reached down and stuck a finger into the dog's ear; it pushed its head against his hand and groaned with pleasure. 'Besides, we've got work to do, haven't we, boy?'

'How's the lambing going?'

'Fine. Most of them are down the hill. Just a couple seem to have wandered off. I'm probably getting too old to keep track of them all.'

'How on earth are you going to find them?'

'Keep looking. I think they might be up towards the north end. That's where I'll head off to first.'

'That could take hours.'

'Maybe all night. I doubt it though. I've never yet known a sheep sensible enough to get itself lost when someone's looking for it.' He snapped his fingers, brought the dog to heel. 'But if you'll excuse me, Mrs Criado, I have to be getting on now.'

'Of course, Sandy. Perhaps see you up here again sometime.'

'Sure.' He coughed. 'I'm sorry for your trouble, Mrs Criado. I hope you can bring your boys next time. I'll show you all the lambs.'

She shrugged. 'That'll depend on the Spanish courts, Sandy. I'm not that hopeful.'

'That's a pity,' he said. 'Folk always tend to stick with their own. No different from here, I suppose.'

He trudged off, the collie darting around him, fluid black like oil. She watched his back for a full minute. Unusual for a man, bringing things home for a living and knowing about birth. Still, men knew how to do that, how to throw you just when you thought you'd got them taped.

God, she couldn't understand the logic, help me understand the logic of him, please. There were times she really thought he'd kill her if she left, times she really thought he'd top himself if she turned him down, times she really thought he meant it when he breenged through the house in a flurry of her clothes, packing her bags and telling her to get out, get out, whore, times when ... her head spun and spun. And then he took her boys anyway. Much the same as killing her.

And they were unhappy. She knew they were unhappy.

A stream cut across the path, and she stopped at the little bridge to wait for McTavish to appear. No sign. She wasn't worried: he was an island dog, he'd fend for himself for a few days then come home. But he was company, and a link to the past, and the boys always asked how he was. She'd rather have him there.

'McTavish! Here boy! Come on!'

He came scuttering out of a clump of trees up to her left and her heart missed a beat. His head was soaked in blood, smeared from his nose, up over his eyes, plastering his ears; as he came closer, she could see the fur around his neck formed into little peaks. And yet he wasn't whining, and he ran easily, so he hadn't been shot by a farmer. Besides, she'd have heard the gun.

He scampered up to her, head down, tail wagging furiously. He turned his back and whipped her legs. Thick sticky strands of white and red and black viscera glistened down his back. Then the smell hit her. Bloody dog. Disgusting habits. Nothing like a good roll in some beast's discarded placenta.

'Jesus, McTavish, you're revolting,' she said. 'You deserve to be shot.' He simpered and sidled up, threatening to jump and lick her hand. She fended him off with her foot. 'Bloody, bloody dog,' she said, and gripped his collar with her fingertips, keeping her hands away from the gore as much as she could. He sat down, always a good way of avoiding going anywhere he didn't want to go, but she slid her other hand under his back legs and hoisted him up.

'Right, McTavish, bath time.'

The dog struggled and she almost lost him, but she tottered to the hand rail of the bridge and lifted him over. He looked at her for a second, pleading, stupid animal, and then gave up the fight and launched himself off her hands. His legs flurried on the way down, he hit the water with a splash and a yelp, and disappeared. She looked down, saw him touch bottom and push up.

The water bubbled and frothed and boiled, turning

a mucky red. Shreds of the afterbirth surfaced, a glutinous scum which swirled momentarily before speeding off downstream. Traces of the stuff clung to her hands, rich and gummy.

Birthblood.

Clean up the mess. Past being a good little woman.

Just clean it up.

McTavish came up for air, got his bearings and swam in a circle, a new game. 'Come on, son, let's go home,' she called. 'We've got things to do.'

In a couple of strokes, he reached the bank, lurching out, ridiculously skinny, and shook himself, an explosion of mercury droplets in the afternoon sun.

Blades

So what the fuck am I doing here? Twelve years since I've been in this place and it's still too busy, too much noise, and toilets that stink and hot water that you can't use because it would strip your skin off. You'd think they'd sort out a water heating problem in twelve years. The people are still the same, girl students dressed in black, and insurance salesmen in grey suits, even the same hairy oddballs, shepherds down from the Isles who won't touch anything except Laphraoig.

It's not them who are the problem, though. It's you. I don't know you any more.

Good to see you, I say. We shake hands, old pals. *How's life?*

Fine, you say.

How many is it now?

Three. One of each.

Ha Ha.

Aye, Daniel's fourteen.

Is he? Fuck, time flies.

I stand with my hands stuffed in my pockets, juggling my unproductive nuts.

No, no children,
not married.
Got close with Anne, though,
lucky escape, eh?
I've never felt the need,
I'm too old now anyway,
thirty-seven,
can you imagine?

Only in situations like this do I make excuses. I am young. I feel as young as I did when we were a team, drinking a dozen Big Whitbreads on Friday nights during the brewery strikes and dancing together at the Savoy, me looking the biz in my greenstitch Wranglers and black velvet jacket but never getting a lumber because I didn't know how. Christ, I couldn't tell you that, going home and falling asleep with the headphones on, waking up to the record pop-pop-popping at the end of the track, ears roasting, while you were away with the blonde or the brunette or the redhead you'd picked up, French kissing and getting your hole. You and Tom and Andy. All of you. Got married to those sweet girls who said 'Yes' when you asked them if they wanted a drink, sweating after Roxy Music's latest had brought you together. All of you. But you were the best. The luckiest.

No. I feel younger. Time has served me well.

I look younger. Than you. Tom says so, sporting a creamy moustache of Guinness.

When are you going to grow old, ya bastard?

I boast about getting into thirty-inch waist jeans again, not since the last year at Uni. Tom has thickened; so have you, I see: well-fed prosperity under a lambswool sweater of grey and lemon diamonds. Mad Andy, still whippet, adrenalin-consuming carbohydrates ...

Listen, do you remember that gendarme,

tried to arrest Andy, threatened to shoot him with a fucking big gun but settled for kicking his arse for pissing up against the plate-glass wall of a restaurant, fancy French diners open-mouthed, showing their half-chewed escargot. Andy ran off, legs flying, arms flying, dick flying, bellowing 'poulet' over his shoulder at the gendarme. Lucky we met him on the way back from the campsite, red mist in his eyes, Swiss Army knife in his hand. He could have cut himself.

I remember that holiday. You and me sat on the boxy little beach at Dinard in the dark and drank duty-free Glenfiddich from the neck and talked a load of shite but it was magical.

It isn't mentioned.

I was the only one sensitive enough to get teenage clinical depression, and did you all suffer for it. Morbid angst of divorced parents and family secrets and insecurity and lack of self-esteem that had me screaming nightmares at three in the morning, saying nothing during whole evenings in the pub having been uncurled like a hedgehog from a corner of my bedroom – 'Davie, Davie, what's up with you?' – by wee sisters who didn't have a clue.

Sex was the real problem with me; you only mentioned it for a laugh. 'Hey boys, do you think Davie's still a virgin?'

Of course I was.

Ha Ha.

I could have killed you: the ease, the chat, the simple invitation, the three-month affair that ended, ended, ended, no pain. I fell, smitten, obsessed with girls who wouldn't fancy me in a million years, wrote 'I love Elizabeth Mackie' in my diary over and over, took half a year to pluck up the courage to ask her out for a meal and felt the world cave in when she'd got herself a new boyfriend the night before, someone better than me, someone interesting.

You set your sights too high, you said.

Are you still setting your sights too high?

Naw,

I'm not interested.

I'm happy,

nice girlfriend,

no ties.

Oh, aye. You look over my shoulder, far off. *Hey boys, she's all right.* Not that far off.

She is. Blonde. Thirty-five-ish. Our tastes grow old with us. She wears a bit too much make-up and glittery earrings and is over-dressed for this pub – black velvet jackets must be making a comeback. But she is. Definitely. All right.

I imagine she sizes you up, measuring possibilities. She looks past me.

See, Davie, that was your problem. Like DB, she was always into big guys, the rugby players. She married Fergus, didn't she? You light a cigarette. *Or Lorna.*

Because she belonged to you. And I felt I belonged

to her, all because of a touch on the arm, a word of kindness. You told me she talked of me; you shouldn't have said that. As far as I knew, she was the first who ever had. You gave me her phone number when you'd finished with her and watched the mayhem I caused, knowing I wouldn't have a thing to say, knowing I wouldn't know what to do. She must have found me torture, my face stuck in a plateful of pasta, my guts grinding for some inspiration and ending up arguing about religion. And blaming you, blameless you. If she goes to Hell, she'll probably spend eternity on that date with me. What a fucking mess I was. 'You've got a lot of hang-ups, Davie,' she said. Serves me right. She was My Best Friend's Girl.

Aye, you never really told me how you got on with her.

Fine,
but everything was too
complicated,
complex,
tense.
You know
how it is,
how everyone would have felt
on an eightsome.

Or on a foursome, just me and Lorna, and you and ?

But I was grateful, you know, for What You Did.

Funny, I'd almost forgotten that, you say. Long time ago. *These things happen.*

Things happen. Lots of things happened. They had to, our team laying waste, hormone-charged weekends when myths were guaranteed. You know everything there was about me, and I wonder what you have done with all that information over the years. Perhaps the butt of nostalgic jokes, always my worst fear. I still avoid situations with the potential for ridicule, feigning headaches, keeping my profile low, so low it's positively fucking subterranean.

Ha Ha

Perhaps you sympathized over long dinners, you all, wives too, candles and best china and crudités followed by a wholesome pasta dish and Vienetta for pud. Or maybe it was your fondue period when Habitat was the place to be and you'd sit there and say, 'Remember Davie, what a nice guy he was, shame about the ...'

Face. The blonde's face swims into view, around Andy's shoulder. You have seen her coming, already prepared. *Do you have a light?* she says, and you half turn, cup your hands around hers to shield the flame and smile, establish complicity in the reprehensible habit, one to start off with. You are lost to us. Tom nudges, winks, and I think, hseck of a guy.

In the Griffin, all of nineteen, standing pishing pure lager, mob-handed on a Saturday night, and that guy at the roller towel talked to you, older, perhaps mid-twenties. You spoke about the rugby, Scotland'd won and wasn't it a great game, and he offered you a cigarette. Piling out, he followed us, sat perched pint in hand on a stool beside you, smiled at your profile and once, just once, patted your knee. You knew what was going on, could feel the thrill of the pick-up in him, and ignored it. Desperate, he was, and when I asked him to leave, he said, 'You can have him,' slammed his pint down so hard it spilled and soaked your cigarette packet, but still you didn't crack, and I sat there with my heart thumping and my knees shaking as the door swung back heavy on those big brass hinges. We all went to The Penthouse, a dive full of dogs, you said, and you lumbered that wee cutter fac Pertick with the spots and the black boob tube. What's a cutter? you asked us.

I didn't know.

The blonde detaches herself, her cigarette already half smoked. You return, smile, *All right, boys?* and, soul of discretion, talk of golf. Tom's a club championship man, won it two years ago, in the top ten for the last six, and you whistle low, can't get your handicap down past ten, and Andy, thrashing the ball around the course with his animal energy, will never see the right side of ninety-five. I have a set of clubs at home, growing old at the back of a cupboard, hardly swung since I bought them with my first pay cheque. No-one to show me the ropes, I tell myself.

I write stories,

and there is a silence, gob-smacked, not much of a social life there Andy supposes, and you draw on your cigarette and mention work. You are all engineers.

The roads you have planned!

The bridges you have built!

The boilers you have stoked!

Do you remember we shared a bed once, pissed at Tom's party, dossing down on a mattress slung slanted on the back-room floor, cot wedged in the corner, billowing out gentle wafts of baby smell, talc and bile and God knows what? I didn't know then. You would now. You smacked your lips all night as you slept, woke me up to the room circling but never seeming to go anywhere, like a spirit-level bubble. I crawled to the toilet and was sick, long hard sick that burned my throat, but I felt better and managed back on my feet and found some girl had crept in beside you, one you'd been chatting up all night and who I thought had left. She slung her arm over your shoulders, and the light outside was coming up and I looked at her dark eyes and she went 'Sshh' and pulled the blankets open behind her. I sagged into bed and she moved closer to you so that our skin wouldn't brush, and I lay awake till seven, the back of my head, my shoulder blades, my spine, my buttocks and thighs and calves and heels tingling at the untouch of her, then fell asleep, and when I woke you'd left. You never mentioned her.

Neither did I.

But I asked where you'd gone. Tom's wife smiled and gave me breakfast and told me not to worry, I didn't need you, I wasn't married to you even though we acted like it sometimes. And why aren't you going out with someone, she asked, you're a good looking guy. She didn't like to see me in your shadow, she said, and anything could happen, there was so much tension between us. I cringed, wanted away from the child in the high chair by the breakfast table and the sun streaming in the window right into my eyes so that I couldn't read her face, not that I would have understood the message anyway. Then Tom came back from getting the Sunday papers and the conversation was dropped and I was relieved, though I spent the next week sleepless thinking about Tom's wife and the girl in the bed and wanked myself stupid.

In the mirror behind you, the blonde looks over. She has a friend, tall, brown haired, a nose slightly hooked, but beggars can't be, and a possibility flashes through my head. I focus on your reflection, notice your crown, thinning, and dismiss the prospect.

You shuffle, impatient, drain your glass and belch softly. It's time for us to go. We drag coats on, jostle to the door, open to the cool night air, and stand just outside, a light drizzle freshening my face as we say our goodbyes.

Well, lads, good seeing you again, you say.

Andy is overcome, *It's been too long boys, what about same day next month?*

Tom agrees, *we were a team, really close,* so important to keep in touch with each other, with the past.

I put my past to the test; I have grown up now, I can cut the crap.

D'you know, in lots of ways we were like lovers.

Behind you, in the light of the pub, it seems there is a wall of faces. One brick in it moves, the blonde gathering up her handbag and kissing her friend, *goodbye,* on the cheek.

You look back at me, peering bland as pork through cigarette smoke.

Maybe you were, those clipped tones, exasperation. *I wasn't.*

Hard cheese, soft cheese

Christopher balanced the plate on his knee, leaned down to rest his wine glass under the garden chair and raised a forkful of salad and barbecued chicken to his mouth. As he did, a bright yellow tennis ball slapped him on the back of the head, a sliver of cucumber missed its mark and left a smear across his cheek as if he had been kissed by a slug, and a chicken wing flew off the plate, landing on the concrete patio. Behind him, the four-year-old giggled. He smiled back, pleased by her good humour: minutes before, she had been miserable and disorientated, having fallen asleep on a warm beach light years away and woken up mysteriously back at home.

'Aw, Joanne, watch what you're doing with the ball. You'll hurt Chris. What do you say?'

'Sorry,' she said.

'It's okay, honey. It didn't hurt,' Christopher said. He lowered his voice conspiratorially. 'Your dad burned that bit anyway. It gives me an excuse not to eat it.'

'Mummy's told you to play with it further up the garden.'

The child grinned at Christopher and obeyed her father, toddling over the patio and onto the lawn. The garden's boundary was marked on three sides by overgrown hedge, and the grass was protected from a faint early-evening chill which blew down the glen and in from the river. The child busied herself throwing the ball over the washing line strung across three poles – a fourth was rusted and halved, like a split dead sapling – and she was soon hot and flushed. She was a pretty child. Christopher thought she resembled her mother.

'More to eat, Chris?' Alan called from the kitchen. He was stacking dishes, stretching cling film over plates and putting food into the refrigerator.

'No thanks. I'm stuffed. That was great.'

'No bother. Least I could do. I've been told all about you cooking for flats full of people in Edinburgh. Mhairi would've starved without you. Then I'd never have met her up here, would I?' His eyebrows raised genially. 'It must have been hell on earth, the way she orders folk around.'

'Yep, that's me.' Mhairi bounced through from the living room, music in her wake: something Handelly or Bachy that Christopher thought a bit soppy. 'I can't cook, you know that. And I can't be as wonderful as I am on an empty stomach. Besides, that's what men are for.' She kissed Alan and helped him with the food. They timed their actions perfectly, weaving together around their kitchen with an intimate synchronicity. They looked happy, suited each other well: the handsome doctor and his beautiful wife. Christopher downed his wine in a single gulp.

'So, it's been nice to meet you finally,' Alan said. 'I think you're the last of her university crowd I've met. She managed to keep in touch with everyone else from the flat.'

Christopher hoped he had rehearsed this well enough. 'Yeah, I know. But I got a research post down south just before your wedding. Last-minute thing. I was sorry to miss it, but I couldn't pass up a job like that.' Alan appeared at his shoulder, knelt to retrieve the wine glass, showed no sign. Should he? 'It's easy to lose touch though, isn't it? Four and a half years gone, just like that.' He snapped his fingers. 'I was really surprised when Mhairi tracked me down last month.'

'The way she described you, I got the impression you were a stuffy college don. You know, bottle-top glasses. Buck teeth.' He called to the kitchen. 'You've been hiding him away, Mhairi.' Christopher shrugged, appropriately modest.

'Of course,' Mhairi said.

'So, what do you do in your spare time?'

Christopher felt at a loss. 'Oh, not much. Not like you two. No gliding. No sailing. I suppose I'm a bit of a layabout.'

'That's not true,' Mhairi protested. 'You go to concerts all the time. You're in a political party, even if it is the wrong one. You've got a very interesting life.'

'Doesn't everyone do things like that?' Alan said.

Christopher wasn't offended, merely humbled, and it didn't help when Mhairi came to his defence, mentioning that he played football and was good at 'ping-pong'. Alan. He was everything Christopher expected and more. Quite a guy. No wonder she'd called it a whirlwind romance at the time, had left so suddenly.

He leaned back, disinclined to talk, and let the evening sun warm his face. Joanne hummed some meaningless, babyish tune while she played her game, the sound apt and familiar, like the buzz of summer insects.

They'd taken a long, sticky drive to the very north-west. His nose practically pressed to the window, Christopher lapped up the names of the villages they passed through – Badcall Inchard sounded like a Mississippi riverboat gambler in an Alan Ladd movie he'd seen once – but his scepticism grew as the villages became more grubby: these were no tourist traps, but were inhabited by people who fished and worked on engines and patched up their lives with corrugated iron.

The car was abandoned at the end of a pitted little track, and Christopher's heart sank at the prospect of what lay ahead: a three-mile trek to the seashore through a bleak landscape of scorched black heather and mushrooms of eroded peat. He was convinced they were lost on some alien world when Alan cheered as they rounded a hill.

'Sandwood Bay!' he cried, arms thrust wide and face beaming.

Pink sand. Acres and acres of peachy-pink sand. The beach curved for perhaps three-quarters of a mile, but it seemed twice as deep as it was wide. A lochan to the south lapped gently in the breeze, and was bounded by an outcrop of pearlescent, raspberry-ripple rock. Cliffs rose on the east and west edges, and the beach was completely deserted.

'Every time I come round that hill, I half expect to see dinosaurs trundling about,' Alan said. Christopher saw his point.

They picnicked in the lee of the huge dune dominating the beach. Cheese and ham sandwiches were passed around, and Joanne was warned by her father not to scramble the dune in case sand fell on the adults below. She stomped off in a huff, pouting her way up and down the dune fifty feet away before she forgot the insult and returned to curl up in her mother's lap like a recalcitrant, exhausted kitten.

The heat intensified towards late afternoon as if to suffocate Christopher for his jokes to Mhairi about bringing thermal underwear and a team of huskies this far north when she first contacted him. The adults fell silent, Mhairi stroking Joanne's hair, Alan reading a book. Christopher looked at their backs, their heads inclining together slightly. He detached himself and wandered off.

He kicked his way across the beach. Minute pieces of grit embedded in the sand had caused a curious, wind-blown effect, each having a tiny mound in its lee, making the terrain crispy underfoot. He clambered onto the red outcrop and squinted out to sea at an oil rig, then counted the sheep on the surrounding hillsides. Mhairi told him years ago that he found too many ways to waste his time, his life. He dribbled some sand through the funnel of his hand.

Fifty-five sheep.

Alan's voice drifted across the beach, calling him. He hauled himself up and returned to the family, fidgety and awkward. Mhairi had forgotten to bring her swimsuit to the beach, and teased him for missing the sight of her sunbathing in her underwear – he watched Alan's back over her shoulder – then chided him, thinking he had wanted to give them time alone. He shouldn't have done that, she said, smiling as she lifted Joanne into his arms to be put in the back of the car. As he hoisted her onto his chest, she squirmed slightly, threatening to waken. He blew gently on her forehead and she calmed.

'Christopher, I'm having tea,' Mhairi called from the kitchen. 'Do you want some?'

'No thanks.' Joanne had picked up a chant, quiet, da – da – di – da – da, lost in some world with someone who listened to her. 'I wouldn't mind a coffee, though.'

'Hard cheese, soft cheese!' Mhairi called, and they both laughed. Alan looked puzzled. 'Private joke,' she explained. 'When we all went shopping together at university, Christopher used to pick the hard, strong cheese and I always bought the soft, mild stuff. It was our catchphrase, wasn't it?'

'Yeah. I think your wife and I are the two people in the world who have least in common.'

'Lucky for me it's not true what they say, then,' Alan said. Mhairi handed Christopher a cup, her fingernail touching the knuckle of his forefinger, and he again felt the strain the sun had managed to dissipate. 'You know, about opposites attracting.'

On the lawn, Joanne howled in anguish. Her ball had taken a cruel ricochet from the washing pole, sailed over her head and disappeared in the tangle of the hedge. Christopher and her parents helped in the search, but it was pointless without knowing which direction the ball had taken and Joanne's sobs gave them no indication of that. They could do nothing, and her distress was compounded by being let down by adults she trusted to make everything right again. Christopher swept her up and wiped her nose with a tissue from his pocket.

'Never mind, it'll be found. Promise. Have you never heard of the Yellow Ball Fairy?' She looked at him as if he were mad, but was intrigued. 'Well, in Fairyland, there's a little yellow fairy who wears yellow dungarees and a yellow hat and yellow clogs and a little yellow and white spotted shirt.'

'Sounds as if he goes to the same tailor as you,' muttered Mhairi as she passed them to go indoors.

'Your mum's cheeky,' he said, and Joanne, her sobbing stopped, nodded her agreement. 'Anyway, this little fairy has a very important job. He has to find the yellow balls lost by all the children in the world. But he's very good at it, and he always finds them. He's very busy though.'

'Why?' she asked.

'Well, he has to find all the yellow balls that have been lost everywhere. So, before he can come to you, he has to find them in ...' – he gulped an exaggerated deep breath and launched off in rhythm – 'Glasgow and Edinburgh and Aberdeen and Dundee and Inverness and Peebles and Greenock and Paisley ...' as he listed them, he sank to his knees, pretending to struggle for air – 'and Motherwell and Kilmarnock and Ayr and Dumfries and Kilmarnock ...'

She chuckled, whacked him on the shoulder. 'You said that twice!'

He collapsed onto his back, Joanne helpless in his arms. 'Oh dear, so I did,' he admitted. 'Maybe there's a lot lost in Kilmarnock.'

The child buried her face in his hair and chortled. Mhairi silently joined them and looked down, the sunlight at her back making her eyes indistinct. Her shape filled his view, excluding everything behind her. She was absolutely still, and he had a sense of somehow being shepherded, brought back to the fold.

He looked at the child's face, at the familiar shape of the nose, at the freckles that belonged to her mother. There were other features, though, which confused him – the blue-greyness of the eyes, a shape of jawline – and he found himself scurrying through dates, events, harsh words, the indignity of begging, all the while desperately trying to explain without flipping the world upside down why he felt he was staring into a mirror.

Joanne sat astride his chest and began to bounce softly up and down, picking up a chorus, louder and louder, filling the garden.

'Hard chee-eese, soft CHEESE!

Hard chee-eese, soft CHEESE!
Hard chee-eese, soft CHEESE!'

There was a crash of china smashing on a tiled floor, and a curse almost like a sob. Joanne flinched. Mhairi raised an eyebrow, shrugged, blew Christopher a private, humourless kiss and turned back towards the kitchen.

Knowing what to say

There wasn't much difference. The same cheap chairs in tweedy fabric. The same emulsioned walls, though peppermint green instead of beige. Industrial carpet. The public sector welcome mat. Posters welcoming parents. Of one sort or another.

– How did it go? Douglas asked.

– It's only eight thirty. Why are you phoning just now? You know it's at eleven fifteen.

– I didn't mean that. I meant the other day.

– Oh.

'Mrs Jarvis? Mrs Jarvis, the interview panel is ready to see you now.'

Rachel pushed her head up and back, and smiled brightly at the secretary. Get in the mood, girl, she told herself. You deserve it. This one is yours. Third time lucky.

She glanced at the man sitting across the coffee table, a nervous, nail-bitten forty-year-old who wore a jumper, for fuck's sake, a jumper to an interview, and who was way too early. Obviously the internal candidate. He was concentrating on his twisting hands, and she felt a rush of sympathy for him, for his oddness. 'Excuse me,' she said, lowering her head to catch his eye: he looked up, startled. 'Good luck. I hope it goes well.'

His chin dropped slightly, he blinked once and went back to his hand-wringing without a word. Rachel wondered how she could possibly work with him: he needed a mother.

– I don't think I can work with you. Not like this. Christ, we're both married. What are we going to do?

Douglas was usually firm and he valued clarity: they had defined the terms of their relationship even before they'd ever slept together. This is just extra fun. A little bit of badness, silliness. We never get involved. We don't interfere with each other's relationships. We are attached, after all. And even in the middle of his orgasms, on the point of saying 'I love you,' he somehow managed mental somersaults that turned it into 'I love this' or 'I love fucking you.' He could have trusted her, she wouldn't have minded. No-one said anything they really meant at times like that.

But she hadn't really expected him to be so lost. She had thought he would cope, the way she intended to cope. They would do something about it ...

– I'm sorry. Look, whatever happens, no-one'll connect us. We've been very careful.

He looked at her, suspicious. He was quiet, and fiddled with his hands. For the first time, she felt he was afraid of her.

– Have you decided? What to do about it, I mean.

What the hell did he think she could do? Blame a miracle and sue the clinic that had done Bill's snip? Hardly likely, the lawyers would want tests. Try to convince him that they had been eating a lot of protein lately, and yes they'd agreed they didn't want children interfering in their lifestyle but wouldn't it be fun, just the three of us ...

– No. I haven't decided yet.

She clipped across the reception hall. Trophy cabinets: good on sport, not much else. The Head stood at the door to his office, hand extended. 'Nice to see you again, Rachel' – did all the candidates get the first name approach? probably – 'come on in. Were running a bit late, I hope you don't mind.'

'Not at all, Mr Alexander.' She took his hand. Firm and friendly and professional; men can be such funny creatures, they easily misinterpret. He led the way in. The man – 'Gerry McNemena, Assistant Head Teacher of ...' – looked up from his notes. Quite fanciable, if you liked his sort. He liked her sort. She noted the slow eyes, from feet to face. She looked good: tiny, smart, neat. Sure of herself. The woman – 'Principal Teacher of ...' – merely smiled and nodded.

She smoothed her skirt over her hips as she sat.

They were seated around a coffee table, studiously and fashionably informal. She held her knees together, slightly to the side, hands folded in her lap. Just like in the *Women into Management* manual, Section Three, The Interview. Don't be sexually assertive it said, between the lines of course. Besides, she'd been in the job long enough to know the signals men claimed they got from women. She'd heard it personally.

– I knew you fancied me.

They were in bed, a hotel they'd used a couple of times. Their first fuck was always slow, as if they were getting to know each other again. Later, they would play in the shower, get more outrageous. Now, though, she felt warm, relaxed. She lifted her head from his shoulder.

– How?

– Och, just the way you smiled. Looked at me. You always sat sort of leaning towards me.

She laughed.

– That's called being friendly, Douglas. Women can be friendly without giving a come on. And we have slightly different body language. You obviously haven't learned it yet.

– So why are you here then? Why are we doing this if you don't fancy me?

– I didn't say I didn't fancy you. I just said I didn't give you any particular messages about it. I don't think I was aware of it until you asked me out for a drink.

– You just don't want to admit it.

He had sounded huffy. She kissed him and said, That's right.

The first question was a dawdle: why you? Why her was easy. She was good. She knew it in that quiet way that refused to threaten anyone, that refused to equate being assertive with being aggressive.

'I think another of my strengths is that I don't take action too hastily. I think it's important that members of my staff could feel they were part of a participative management. In my temporary management posts, I feel that I involved the staff well in all the major initiatives which we had to undertake, and that included a clear process of evaluation, planning and monitoring at every stage ...'

They seemed impressed so far. Mrs PT smiled, Gerry raised his eyebrows appreciatively as he scribbled notes. She drifted a bit in her head, but she'd prepared well: just a matter of the requisite number of buzz words.

'... of course, consultation is all very well, but a manager has to take responsibility: the buck stops there ...'

– Look, I'm sorry, I don't know what to do.

– That's okay. It's difficult for you, I know.

– It's just ... I'm sort of unsure. Torn. I don't want to leave my kids.

– Or your wife. It's okay to say it. I don't want to leave my husband.

He had that scared look again, but there was something else, like he'd made his mind up, that he wasn't unsure at all and he'd found a way that suited him. He just didn't know how to tell her. She could understand.

– I just don't see why you did it.

– Did what?

– I told you I hadn't put a condom on. You pulled me into you. I just don't know why you did that.

– Oh God, Douglas, no. I can't explain it.

– I think you have to. Explain it.

– What difference does it make? You'll be all right. I promise.

– I need to know.

Having to think for them both gave her a headache. Did he know how he overpowered her, wore her down? She had watched a television programme the night before. The Gulf War. Nineteen-year-old American soldiers bulldozing sand into trenches filled with Arab men. Burying them alive.

– Okay. Just once, I wanted you inside me. I wanted your semen up me. I wanted to be able to put a finger inside myself and smell you. Not rubber.

He shook his head. The bastard didn't even have the decency to understand.

– And do you know how I felt, Douglas? Eh? Lonely. I realized it didn't matter. You and Bill and every other man. It doesn't matter. There's no difference. You all just make a mess. Don't worry, I'll clean it up.

– Are you going for it?

– Yes. But it's my decision. Not yours. Your feelings don't even come into it.

He had looked offended.

'Thanks very much, Rachel.'

– Thanks very much.

– Don't mention it.

He left her room. She waited until he would have got to the end of the corridor. Then she threw the blackboard duster at the closed door. It left a perfect, white rectangle where the back of his head would have been. Her hand trembled.

Mrs PT raised her eyes above her notes. 'Rachel. Nice to meet you. I'd like to think ahead, in a year's time when Mr Alexander asks you how your department is doing and you have to show him some measure of your success. Could you tell me what indicators you would use to measure a department's effectiveness?'

Her belly lurched: last night's wine, probably. She clicked into the answer easily enough. Regular review, at least annual. Departmental targets drawn from areas of identified needs. Close monitoring of classroom teaching, done in as supportive a way as possible. Keeping her mind on the answer helped quell her stomach, which settled into a smouldering cramp she could cope with because it wasn't all that different from her period. She could put it aside. Just put it aside. Until later.

Of course, she shouldn't have drunk. Not after just getting out. And especially not alone. But Bill had to have his tennis club boys' night. It was regular.

She'd got a video and watched a film about a man in love with a hairdresser, and they got married and he danced for her around the shop to an Algerian tune and they fucked gently and secretively as she cut the customers' hair. When the hairdresser had felt that she couldn't ever be any happier, she'd thrown herself into the river, and the man who'd always loved her died inside and closed the shop.

She wept so much she wondered if it was hormonal. Probably. That morning, her breasts had ached and her nipples had felt solid, like concrete. She had gritted her teeth when Bill rolled over and slid his arm through hers to fondle her. His cock pressed against the back of her thigh and he pushed it between her legs, murmuring 'come on, come on'. No, she'd said, I'm not feeling well, and he'd tutted and got ready for work without saying any more and without kissing her.

Now, her sweater was damp with tears, and wine and more wine just made her worse. She had needed a kiss. She needed to be held. She felt a space around her, a vacuum that had to be filled. It had to be filled with something. She carried on crying.

She pulled her legs up onto the sofa and wriggled out of her jeans and pants. Her vagina looked no different. No reason why it should. She'd worried about having to explain being shaved, but they didn't need to do that these days. She inserted a finger, feeling as deep as she could to find any sign of what wasn't there any more. There was some pain, but it wasn't that that made her cry.

A gel, harmless stuff, to induce delivery of a pre-term foetus, the doctor told her. Overnight stay. Nothing to worry about. Occasional risks of infection, retention of placenta. She'd left it late, but not too late. Just be careful over the next week or so. Keep an eye out. For bleeding.

– Am I doing the right thing? she'd asked him, and he'd looked at her like she was from another planet and mumbled something about how he was sure she'd discussed that in Counselling. He had shuffled away, writing something on a clipboard.

– Am I doing the right thing? she'd asked the midwife, and the woman, fifty and greying and a mother of three, all married and a grandchild on the way, she'd said

proudly, sat on the edge of the bed and put an arm around her and told her yes, of course.

When it was over and she was returned to the ward, that midwife was off duty, and another one gave her a cup of tea and apologised because she had a baby up from labour suite with complications. She would look in when she could.

'Well, Rachel, that concludes the formal part of the interview. Now, we know that you might leave the room and feel there was something else you wanted to say, or that one of the questions didn't cover ground which you think essential. So, is there anything else you'd like to add?'

They each smiled encouragingly. She had done well, she knew. A storming finish, girl, and it's yours. She'd done a lot of that. Finishing.

The ache in her belly dislodged and eased. The room swam, just for a second, and she felt as if she were filled with warm liquid. Hot tea, perhaps. It shifted down, filling her insides with a definitely pleasant sensation.

She must have fallen asleep, or passed out, and she woke around midnight. She was on the floor, back against the sofa. The video had finished and switched itself off: some fat men played darts and a commentator squealed.

'Well, yes. I think I really should ...'

She felt sick and dizzy. She lifted her hand from between her legs: her fingers were scarlet with blood, but it hadn't been a heavy bleed. There was a deep purple patch on the carpet, the size of a half-wine-glass spill.

Raising standards of attainment. Yes. Gather the thought, get it out. Heads like the idea of raising standards of attainment. But she suddenly felt a dampness in her knickers, just a trickle. She wished she'd worn more than a liner, just in case.

'I ... an important issue ...

Her head lost it. All her concentration was on what was happening to her, to her insides. She closed her eyes and tried to focus, but couldn't grasp the important issue which was so important, it was vitally important, it was – she gave up and sighed, and the movement of air into and out of her lungs seemed to release something inside her, and the warmth flooded downwards.

'Sorry, I ...'

She had moved the rug over the stain, would get it tomorrow. Bill would be back soon. She didn't want him to see her unsteady on her feet, didn't know how she would react if he put his arms around her.

She might even tell him. He thought she was at a conference. He would be hurt by the lie.

Besides, she had to get to bed. To sleep. She had a big day ahead.

Christ, it must be showing by now, they must see it soon. Fuck. She could feel the wetness between her thighs, could feel the metallic slippiness of blood soaking into the seat cushion. Her fingertips turned icy cold and she shivered once.

'Rachel,' said the Head. 'Are you all right? You've gone a terrible colour. Can I get you anything?'

She couldn't tell them. They had to find out sometime, but she couldn't tell them. The flow was easing, but her buttocks were sticky and she was sleepily mortified at the thought that the blood would begin dripping onto the Head's carpet. She couldn't move, knew that if she tried to raise herself onto her legs she would make some sort of a fool of herself. Just sit here, then. They seemed to be realising something anyway: Mrs PT was on her feet moving towards her, but really slowly, she thought. She would just sit here and rest and close her eyes and think, think about what to tell them when they found out.

Muezzin

Early morning. You stand at the entrance. Stone arch after stone arch is thrown up and over like the rib cage of some giant worm, and you're a wee boy again, sitting in front of your mother's dressing table: you held her long, thin-handled vanity glass up to the big mirror and watched the gilt frame reflected over and over again into infinity, curving out of your sight, out of your reach.

You're gawping.

Two Americans push past, fat, sleek, brightly clothed in the genuine articles. 'Duane', the woman says, 'look at these', and she fingers some scarves. The shop owner looks at you, his one eye casts up and he mouths 'One dollar, one dollar,' towards the roof.

It's not hot yet. Not crowded. The guys at the shop entrances are cool, relaxed, all wearing the same grey or beige trousers and short-sleeved white-checked shirts your mother bought you from her catalogue in the 1970s. Their welcomes are real, and they don't try to usher the few stragglers inside. You meander up and in.

It's not what you expected. It's cool, grey, not so different from Saint Sofia. You find yourself surrounded by a dozen brassware shops, like Santa's grotto, vases the size of tubas, gold-Christmas light.

It'll be a bit intimidating for Fraser, says Janice, and she wouldn't feel comfortable bartering: what on earth do you say? But you go, she says, you'll enjoy it. We'll stay at the hotel. Just make it early 'cos we have to get the transfer to the resort.

'Apple tea, sir?'

'Pardon?'

'Apple tea? Come in. Come in.'

He's small, barely five foot two, and his face seems made of dark latex. It squelches itself up into a grin, broken toothed and roguish and totally honest. He bows a little, his hand gesturing elegantly inside his shop.

KARABATAK. He sees you looking up at the sign, and gestures at his heart.

'Me. Selahattin Karabatak.' He bows again. 'How do you do?' he asks, and bows once more, and you can't help thinking of Peter Lorre.

'Fine, thanks.'

'Please. Come in. I give you apple tea.'

'No, thanks. I'm just looking.'

He pouts a bit: you've offended him, but not much. 'I not try to sell you anything,' he says. 'Just come in. For tea. Sit on my carpets.'

He sells carpets. They fill the windows, rolled up loosely, showing eighteen inches of draped-down pattern like some gorgeous woman's stocking top. And they *are* gorgeous. The colours are dusky, deep, the patterns swoosh curvaceously or slice at geometric angles.

'They're lovely,' you say, nodding up at the rolls as you step in.

'Ah, yes, very good quality. I give you good price.'

'No. No thanks. I don't have any money on me.'

'I show you anyway.'

He flutters at the back of the shop, brings you a small, hot glass of strong apple-tasting stuff, thick and syrupy: 'All natural,' he says. He heaves down a roll, flicks it out. You're perched on a stool and almost fall back to avoid being caught in the eye. 'Beautiful, yes?'

It is. The geometry is perfect, almost fractal, and the hues are of fields and caves and clay. He pulls the pile apart, shows you the double knots. 'My family make these,' he says, with evident pride which might or might not be real. He turns it, heaving it round like a boat at mooring, and says, 'What do you see?'

It's changed colour. The clay is now rust, the field is now olive oil, the cave is now slate. You nod, 'Clever,' and he's pleased.

'Ah, but this just wool on wool. Now silk.'

He sweeps a curtain aside. There is a light panel on the wall, covered by a dowdy scrap of beige cloth. He flourishes once with his left hand. The shop goes almost pitch and you wonder for an instant if there are cut-throats behind you, but he flourishes again with his right and the panel flickers on and the silk comes alive, shimmering swoops and swishes and curves like some backlit oriental dancer. You feel your mouth hanging open.

'You like it.' Statement, not question.

'Yes. Very much.'

'I give you good price.'

'No, no,' you say as he switches on the naked bulb overhead and unhooks the carpet, gossamer fine and handkerchief-tiny, from the frame. 'I don't have any ...'

'You ever see magic flying carpet?'

He launches it into the air, and it does. The bloody thing flies. It hangs on the meagre thermals of the shop, spins leisurely above your head, hovers, flapping its silvery fringes like flagella to bring itself floating down gracefully, surrendering on the floor at your feet.

'How much?' you ask, and the man grins with no hint of triumph.

'I said I give you good price.' He picks it up, begins to roll it, sandwiched between two huge sheets of tissue paper. 'You not pay duty at airport. This is work of art. Five hundred pounds.'

Shit, you think. Janice will never go for this: a two-by-one foot scrap of cloth that she'll probably think looks best on the bathroom floor. We can't afford it, she'd say.

'No, I'm sorry, I don't have enough money. My wife wouldn't let me, anyway.'

He grues at the word, outraged that the mention of a woman should intrude in the bartering of men. You see dusty camels at the oasis, the romance of sunsets and Tuaregs. You are Lawrence. Or at least Peter O'Toole.

'Okay, okay,' he says, 'four hundred fifty pounds. My last offer.'

It isn't – or wouldn't be – but you say, 'Do you take Visa?'

He is disappointed. He wanted more of a fight. You instantly become a flabby foreigner, an infidel, but he likes you anyway.

'Visa, yes. But I have to pay commission. If you have cash, I make it four hundred thirty.'

'No. I don't have cash.' You have already taken your card out. It flexes sweatily, eagerly, in your hand. 'None at all.'

He is trying very hard. He offers to take you to the bank, get cash out, no problem and you save and he saves. You lean forward, are about to say you don't have time, and his hand clasps the card and he is off, the roll of carpet underneath his left armpit, out of the shop, saying 'Come, come,' and he is away down through the bazaar, parting the smells of thick pastries and syrupy sponges and smouldering kebabs. You lose sight of him, then spot the tiny gold oblong of plastic, raised above his head, leading you, showing you the way.

He dashes out into the sunshine, through the early morning traffic, between the gridlocked flatbed trucks and three-wheeler corrugated delivery vans. You watch him hurdle a tiny goat being driven by an old man who shouts at him. You are breathless, fall behind, but he keeps your card up and you watch it part the crowded pavements.

The bank is a good five-minute run. It is on the ground floor of a concrete office block, indistinguishable from any bank anywhere in the world. Grey carpet, lilac tweed chrome-framed chairs, perspex on pine. It is cooler, air conditioned, as if money were a Western European concept refrigerated and imported here to the edge of Asia.

'I ask if we can get money,' he says. He ignores the queue of suits, simply parks himself at its head and talks around the woman who is paying her bills. You shuffle behind him, not knowing whether to nod an apology to the others or ignore them. You opt for the latter: no-one seems to notice.

The teller holds a hand up to stop his chatter, finishes with the woman, then turns a dazzling smile on him.

She is young, perhaps twenty-two. She has blonde hair and dark eyes and a Byzantine face. Her clothes are standard bank uniform – navy skirt, black tights, no doubt sensible shoes if you could see behind the desk – but her white blouse peeps slightly wide between the third and fourth buttons and a curve of lace nestles a breast of unblemished toffee skin. Your knees have an adolescent urge to buckle beneath you.

She looks once at you, then back to the shop keeper, nods, says 'Of course,' in a language you don't understand. Your card disappears into her hand, she turns to swipe it through a machine. The shop keeper grins at you – he has solved your financial problems at one fell swoop – but you are watching the line of her jaw as she leans forward to punch some buttons.

'You like her?' This time a question.

You jump slightly, caught out, swither for a second between honesty or offence. 'She's very pretty,' you admit. 'A beautiful girl.'

'Very beautiful.' Then he takes your shoulder, angles his head, speaks low. 'You want meet her?'

You may have misheard, but the images are already thundering through your brain. You shake your head, 'No, no, I'm married, my wife would ...' and slice your hand across your throat.

'No problem. You leave wife shopping. You, me, we meet later. Go to discotheque. I know this girl.'

'Look, no, I can't, I'm leaving ...'

But he is already making the arrangements with her, his voice animated, his gestures indicating you, her, both of you. She listens, blushes, turns to you. You throw your eyes up, shrug innocently, half smile.

'I explain. You nice man. Take her for dinner tonight. I know restaurant. Okay?'

'But I can't speak to her.'

'I be there.'

This is preposterous, you think. The girl, though, nods softly. 'She likes you,' he says. 'She likes people.' She says something that sounds sweet, genuine. Your mouth is dry.

She passes a small white slip of paper for your signature, but doesn't bother comparing it with your card. She counts out money – you lose track of the millions of lira – and the wad of notes is gently pressed into your hand. Her skin is cool as her fingers curl around yours for a second: you imagine you can feel her fingerprint. She leans forward and speaks to the shop keeper while she looks at your eyes. Hers are chestnut brown.

He laughs. 'She says not to cheat you. You are nice. She says you look honest.' He takes the money from you, peels off some notes – 'I only take three hundred and eighty' he says – and gives you an inch-thick pile back. 'Okay?' he says to the girl, and she nods.

You blunder away from the desk, out into the daylight, somehow managing a coy wave to the girl as you leave, the shop keeper grinning, elbowing you in the ribs. You don't feel it. Something is swimming in your head.

'We meet here', he says, 'later.'

He presses the roll of carpet into your arms, darts off backwards, smiling. 'You are my friend,' he shouts as he disappears. You are left hemmed in between a row of Fiat taxis and a huge wall, each honey sandstone block the size of a small bungalow. They stretch upwards, out of sight, curving over your line of view. You feel giddy, and reach out a hand to steady yourself.

You are thirty-five. You are married, with a son. Your waistline is getting a bit too round for football. The mortgage rates have just gone up and you have had sleepless nights about it. You have nothing this girl could want.

It's a fit-up, obviously. Get you to some den up the Taksim Square, candles and raki, the girl flirting, laughing, the shop keeper making bad jokes, nudge-winking you as you get drunker, a few thugs beat you up, rob you, take your money, your traveller's cheques, your passport, having to go to the consulate, admit stupidity.

And Janice. Christ.

A taxi takes you back to the hotel. The room is still in semi-darkness, the muslin curtain pulled across the open French window. It's stifling. Most of the heat radiates from the warmth of the bed, the warm-woman smell of Janice.

She stirs, rolls over.

'What time is it?'

'Just before ten.'

'Mmm. Couldn't open my eyes. How'd you get on?'

'Oh, okay.' The carpet feels suddenly heavier. 'Bought a wee rug. Real silk.'

'Great. How much was it?'

'Quite dear, but it's lovely.'

'How dear?'

'Just under a hundred.'

You are at an edge, could fall either way. She knows you are reckless. Sometimes it annoys her.

'Oh well. You haven't bought much yet. As long as you like it.'

Sometimes it's part of your charm.

'Where's Fraser?'

'Oh. Downstairs. In the creche. He woke me up about half-eight.'

'We'll have to get packed. Do you want me to get him?'

'Yeah. In a minute.' She stretches her arms over the sheet, extends them outward, towards you. 'Give us a cuddle.'

She is warm and soft, but there is a power in her arms. She turns her head away – 'haven't brushed my teeth yet' – and you nuzzle your face into her neck, lie along her length. You are still with her.

'Need to get the boy,' you say into her shoulder.

'That'd be great. Thanks.'

You disentangle yourself. Her hand runs down your arms, catches the tips of your fingers, gently holding you back for a moment.

'Love you,' she says.

'Thanks,' you say.

The lobby of the hotel is awash with suitcases. A young woman, English – Essex, you reckon – is calling out names. She is flat chested and heavy hipped, wears beige bermudas, a navy polo top, red 'AirHols' embroidery on the breast pocket. Pink women with cheesecloth tops and flowery skirts answer her, their husbands bleary-nosed from last night's drinking, their children fractious, burned, bored. You squeeze your way through, past reception, past the overpriced telephone kiosk, through a fire door, its bar handle broken, hanging loose, out to the playground. Fraser is the only child there. He sits on a swing, gently tipping himself forward and back, humming a song. He is supervised by a pimply boy, eighteen maybe, dressed in the same navy top and beige shorts. He slumps at a pine bench-cum-table, feet up. He squints at you.

'Hi there,' he says. 'How are you?'

'Fine, thanks.'

'Good. Last day then?'

'Yes.'

'So what do you think, then?' He thinks you have not understood, doesn't realize you don't want to speak to him. 'You know. Istanbul?'

You wonder what he wants. What would be best to say. 'Janice thinks it's a bit dirty,' you say. 'We're looking forward to Kusadasi.'

He seems placated. 'That's what everyone thinks. Bus leaves at four-twenty. Okay?'

'Yeah. Fine. We'll be ready.'

'Great. Enjoy your day then.' It's all he can muster, slouches onto his feet. 'I'll go now. Seeing you're here to look after the little fella.'

'Sure. Bye.'

You slink up behind Fraser, grab him around the waist. 'Gotcha,' you say, and he chuckles. 'How're you doing?' He is still in his pyjamas.

'Fine,' he says. 'I'm going to be a pilot when I grow up.'

'That's good. I thought you wanted to be a lawyer, though.'

'Yeah. That too.'

'And a professional rugby player?'

'Uh-huh.'

You begin to swing him, gently. He leans his head back, looks at you.

'What did you want to be, Dad?'

'When I was your age?' You reach back, find nothing. 'I can't remember,' you say, and feel frightened.

'My Daddy,' he says, and giggles. You give a heave on the plastic seat, push him further away from you.

'That's right,' you say.

In the distance, you hear the call from the mosque, nasal, piercing, summoning the faithful. It ululates through the pale blue air.

This is not your life.

'Push me higher, Dad.' He picks up a chant, 'Higher, higher.' So you do.

It goes up, comes down.

Goes up, comes down.

The links in the chain begin to rattle, and at the top of the push they go loose and look like scribbles of black felt tip against the sky. 'Enough, enough!' he shouts, and he starts to cry and waggle his legs about.

You keep on pushing.

The bus fare down the tubes

I'm sitting quietly, sipping my pint of Caffreys, and I know I've done it now. Genuinely, truly, by fuck, fucked up good and fucking proper, and all I can do is stare at young Tracy the barmaid, heavy curls like those tendrilly things in the Botanic Gardens. She looks out from them at me and I want to take her deep into the darkness of the loam and push her short black skirt up over her thighs and bury my cock right up her youthful knowing cunt and fuck her 'til her nose bleeds.

She says 'hello, funny seeing you midweek', and 'how are you doing anyway?' though she doesn't hang about for much of an answer.

Aw Tracy. How am I? Well might you ask, pet. Load of shite actually. Has been for quite a while. And it's not going to get much better.

When I left my wife, I packed a suitcase. Enough shirts and ties and trousers and a jacket to keep myself in school uniform for a week, and moved out, off to my mum's on the bus; a week would do, I reckoned. It was a single-decker, hardly more than a minibus, and the only seat was behind the driver, this shaven-headed guy with an expensive t-shirt who smoked despite the signs on all the windows. He drove along behind another bus, a double-decker with an advert for a lingerie shop plastered huge on the back, facing us. He leaned over his shoulder, stabbed his cigarette in the direction of the black-and-white girl, beautiful, sexy, legs apart, almost showing what nice girls shouldn't. 'Fuck's sake', he said, 'cannae drive wi' a hard-on.' I laughed, said, 'must cause a few accidents', and he told me about the late-night slags who have their bus fare but offer him his hole because they like it that way anyway. Eighty-five pence worth.

Christ, the things we do for love.

My mother wasn't pleased to see me, but wouldn't ask, just told me to put my stuff in the spare room. 'Are you staying long?' she asked. I didn't know then, but that was six months ago. I do now.

Work didn't go well today. No, no. Not well at all. Not gone well. My third warning in a month from baldy-heided bastard boss for being late, and no doubt he's sniffing last night's boozer from me. What the fuck does he know? What the fuck? And my second row in a week from Mizz Shiny Shoes, Mizz Twinkle Toes, for not having my exam marking done.

I have better things to do, Mizz McMenamin.

Like watch my life go down the nearest fucking stank, bitch-boss.

And neither could my appointment with Fat Carol from Fourth Year be described as a roaring success. Flab and tits round her waist. 'How're yoo, Mr Campbell?' she says through a gobful of chewing gum, and she sounds like a cow pulling its hoof out of mud.

'I'm fine, Carol. Nice to see you. How have you been getting on in Home Economics? Sorted out that wee problem with Mrs Gideon?'

Carol sits on a pupil's desk. She wears a skirt far too short, white tights. She has thighs like dead dolphins.

Oh Christ, the sight of what I do.

What do they call those white dolphins?

Six months. Fuck's sake.

But it definitely wasn't an affair.

VERY ATTRACTIVE FEMALE 31 yrs 5'2". Long blonde
hair and sexy eyes! Likes travel, wine & dining.
Seeks males ...

Etcetera

Etcetera

Etcetera

Some pathetic contact inserted between the domestic appliance small ads and the Masonic notices. Fantasy a phone call away.

Aye, right.

But you get through. Eventually.

How could she call that an affair? Come on. Shagging around, machismo, I'd maybe even go for menopause. But unfaithful? I don't feel guilty, it just happened. I got bored, the same triangulation of legs, the same fucking geometry time after time after time.

Oh God, for something different.

The geometry of Tracy. She stands at the beer pump, spine curved slightly, hips swung back, one leg bent forward. Take an artist's brush, slip it in black ink, smooth three lines flowing down parchment like some slinky breathless Japanese letter for *fuck only me*, and you've described her.

How can you be expected to resist something new, alive? That second or two when you kiss a stranger for the first time, and you wait, tasting the same air, and it tingles around your mouth and down your throat. And then she moves on top of you, arches her back to feel your cock pushing deeper into her, sweats when she fucks you and you have to clamp your hand over her mouth to stop her screaming and when you're finished she looks at you with blurred eyes and someone else's face.

Of course it's wrong. That's why it's necessary, for Christ's sake.

She was just some desperate wee woman from the Saturday papers.

When the wife asked, I couldn't explain: the credit card bill with the hotel name she'd never heard of; the condoms in my shaving bag; the last-call facility we'd just got on our exchange, and the woman's voice she pretended to be a wrong number to. She'd spent months gathering the evidence, reluctantly, each bit almost by accident, hoping it would all fall into place, a different place from the one she was in.

I think I'll go and eat worms.

So I left.

Or was chucked out.

I can't remember.

Aye, my life's a mess, and poor big Carol didn't know what to think.

I couldn't help her there. Hardly know myself these days.

No-one likes Carol. She's loud and fat and common, though she's completely blind to her inadequacies. She can't understand why she's shunned, why she hasn't any friends.

'Take it easy, Carol, ' I say.

'But why umma no happy, like?' she pleads. 'Why wullnae people like me?'

'Relax, Carol, relax. I'll relax you.'

And something's going way wrong here and I'm moving in like a lounge lizard on this flabby lassie and my hand's on hers stroking it ever so solicitously and my other hand fondles the hem of her skirt and slips easily up the snake-skin nylon and her fingers are soft and boneless like uncooked sausages while I lean towards her and smell the pickled onion corn chips she's eaten for lunch and I try to kiss her cheek feeling marshmallow spongy against my lips.

And I feel a tear in my eye.

And my nose is about to drip, fuck it.

Fuck it.

She's wearing tights.

A sexless Sindy doll, without the anorexia.

I whip my hand down from under her skirt and she looks at me, 'whit wizaw that aboot?' and I shake my head because I'm buggered if I know.

'Trying to comfort you, Carol. Gotta bit carried away.' She looks green, her mouth hangs open, glaikit. I might have got away with it, just, but then I fuck myself right up. 'No need for a fuss, eh?'

Her big ugly face reddens across her cheekbones,

and her eyebrows furrow. 'Yoor a durty auld bastart,' she says. 'Yoor feart Ah'll tell. Well ah fuckin wull, ah wull.' She heaves herself off the desk and makes for the door. I try to grab her arm but she twists out of it, 'piss off,' she says, and she's gone. Away. Somewhere.

I sit at the desk, knowing that's it, and my career would be flashing before my eyes if I wasn't so exhausted and if my head didn't hurt so much.

Maybe she won't say anything.

Maybe I can deny it; after all, her word against mine, and the system's to blame anyway, putting me in a position like this without training, guidance, protection. I could be accused of anything, anything at all, and they don't even pay me for it, voluntarily putting my future on the line to help one fat sad wee case who cannae cope with real life, wee bitch turning on me like that after everything I've done for her ...

But Tracy is gorgeous. She bends to fetch a bottom-shelfer beer, movement like a skater collecting roses from the surface of the ice.

I'm away again.

A wee game. Did you know you can change 'love' to 'lust' in only two moves, one letter at a time?

First step's 'lose'. Second's 'lost'.

Amazing, eh? Amazing. So I've decided. I'm going to brazen it out. When I reach the staff room, Mizz McMenace is holding court. Something about professional standards, can you believe it? Poor old Anderson doddering down the corridor again, soup stains on his tie apparently. Fuck fuck fuck fuck fuck fuck off. I wonder if she's getting shagged and if I could possibly bring myself to but, come on, a man's got to have his dignity. Christ, I'd rather shag her briefcase. Someone changes the topic to last night's *Star Trek* and I annoy them by picking holes in the plot again, like where did that alien in the shuttle craft come from when it'd just been left for dead by the good Doctor Crusher on her mortuary slab, and I'm called a cynic and it's just escapism, and the phone rings.

For Mizz Chirpy Chops.

I keep the conversation up – the old lot were better, had a more realistic attitude to the sexual tensions on a lonely seven-year mission – but out of the corner of my eye she's looking at me, definitely is, the Mizz is menacing me, like what right does she have, self-righteous bitch bitch bitch bitch, and the phone's down and she's round the back of me and says the baldy-heided bastard boss would like to see us right away, only she refers to him as the rector, and me she calls by my surname, Mister Campbell no less, and everyone wonders what I've done to deserve such formality, but I know, don't I?

Christ I can tell she's loving this even though she doesn't know what's going on yet. 'He sounded really angry,' she says. 'Do you know what this is about?' And I say no, haven't a clue. The weans are swilling about, bouncy wee kids in perky little maroon blazers who smile at us until they see Mizz McMurder's stony face.

I'm not taking this, no no no way am I being marched along this bloody corridor like Master Naughty Bottom and who the hell does she think she is judging me. No-one but no-one can do that.

She even takes my elbow.

Propels me through the last fire door.

It's Take Your Pick time, I'll tell you. To the right, the administration wing, complete with baldy-heided bastard boss' domain, no doubt sitting cozy with Carol.

Light shines from the left, the main doors.

EXIT

So I just peel off, just shuffly-toe toward that door and FREEDOM, FREEDOM, feeling so proud, like me in control, just move towards those big glass doors and up up and away from Mizz McMenstruate, and she doesn't like this one bit.

'Mr Campbell', she says, 'Mr Campbell we have to see the rector', but she can't exactly grab me because there's all sorts of wee ones around and the jannie's looking perplexed by my face and the way her voice is getting shriller and shriller and I'm out the doors and I start walking so cool down the driveway it slopes down and I'm strolling and picking up speed a bit sort of walking fast and I hear her screaming at me and I pick my heels up and run run run run run run fast as lightning fast as the wind fast as a lost soul out the back gates of hell and my jacket's bumping up and down and my classroom keys go flying but fuck them and a few bits of chalk and a red pen out my top pocket and I'm out those gates and the sky's blue and my get out of jail card's worked its magic!

But what do I do now?

What about Tracy, beautiful Tracy of the grey-blue eyes and long legs and tendrilly hair? I can tell she's wondering what I'm doing in the pub of a Wednesday afternoon, getting guttered instead of earning my honest crust in front of my third year bampots.

Sold the jerseys.

I check my pockets, see what's left for the old Caffreys top-up. Well what do you know? Eighty-five pence.

Not enough for my bus fare home. Wherever that is.

Besides, they'll be waiting for me.

Tracy. I'll maybe see her later.

Christ, I've got it. Belugas.

Imagine me remembering that.

Fucking belugas.

Fish in the sea

Honestly, I couldn't help it. There he was, nodding off, his paper propped up and this really interesting article facing me. He sat funny, his legs crossed really carefully, his right sock resting on his left knee: not the shoe, not the trouser leg, very definitely the sock. Even half asleep, he left a good nine inches of space all round him. Prissy bugger, I reckoned.

Look, it was an interesting article. On violence and film noir in the 1990s. Poser, me. Did a film studies course at College last year, and I know every Tarantino script off by heart. Not my favourite, though. *Twelve Angry Men*, now there's a film. Henry Fonda, Lee J. Cobb, 1957. I could name six of the others, but I always forget the last four. Sidney Lumet directed it though. Impressive, eh?

So then he woke up. He blinked twice to clear his head and rejoin the planet. The train was leaving Crossmyloof, which seemed to annoy him. He flipped the paper closed to read the front page.

Okay, okay, I shouldn't have, but it was too tempting. 'I'm sorry', I said, 'I was reading that.' I tried to soften it a bit, reached over to touch his shin.

'I beg your pardon?' He looked up over his paper at me. I don't think he'd noticed me before.

'Your newspaper. The page facing me. I was reading it.' He didn't seem to grasp my meaning, but the man in the beige raincoat sitting next to him twigged and looked away, shuffling in his seat. By this time, I was feeling a bit naughty. 'Could you turn it back please?' I said, ever so sweet, and I opened my eyes wide and smiled at him. He was okay, maybe mid-thirties, but just so uptight. A bit of teasing wouldn't hurt.

'I'm sorry ...' he said. 'I don't think ... how can you? ... it's my paper you know.'

So I sighed slightly and cocked my head. I touched

his leg again and felt him jump through the material of his trousers.

'It's not too much to ask, surely? I thought you were asleep. Besides, I was positive you wouldn't mind.'

I could see him debating, saying damn it, what's happening here? He wanted to say I had no right. He wanted to fold the paper to a new page, stick it up in front of his face and pretend to read. Instead, he found himself looking down the front of my denim jacket at the V of my throat, way down between my breasts. He looked up and I caught his eyes, and he knew I knew.

'I'm sorry ...' he said again. He unfolded his legs and the paper slipped onto the floor of the carriage, unravelling and ending up in a scruffy heap.

So I laughed. 'You didn't have to go that far! My wee brother does that.'

'Does what?'

'Spoils things so that no-one else can have them. He puts tomato ketchup on his chips because he knows I don't like it, then leaves half of them. Drives me wild.'

'Oh, I'm sorry' – it was quite sweet the way he couldn't stop saying that, even if he was a bit of a nerd – 'I'll ... here ... I ...' He gathered up the sheets, ruffling them into some order, and offered me the bundle.

'It's okay now,' I said. 'The train's just coming in to Central.' I pushed the paper away, my fingertips on the back of his hand. 'And please stop apologizing.'

And that was it, as far as I was concerned: just a wee bit of misbehaving. The train braked and I stood up, collected my rucksack from the luggage rack. I smiled, said 'Goodbye,' over my shoulder, went down the carriage to the doors. I had the impression he was standing there behind me, watching me as I left, but it wasn't my problem. I hit the ticket office – I was off to London to see some of my pals – and then had a while to wait. I like railway stations; there's always something interesting, like down-and-outs who'll tell you life stories you wouldn't believe, or young guys selling the *Big Issue* who try to chat you up. So I settled down on the red plastic seating, looking up at the departures board and generally watching the world go by.

And all of a sudden, there he was again, right in front of me. 'Hello there ...' he said, 'I was wondering ...' I could see his chest heaving, he was like really nervous. 'The article you were reading, would you like the paper?'

So I'm feeling suspicious, like Mum says never speak to strangers, and the guys in collars and ties are the worst. In my experience anyway. 'No,' I said. 'I said it was okay.'

'It's just I don't mind. And it does look interesting. It was the film article, wasn't it?' I nodded. 'I teach Media ... at the College. Do you like films?'

Corny chat-up line, I reckoned, but I relaxed 'cause he wasn't much of a threat. He looked as if he was psyching himself up to jump off a cliff. 'Yes, I do.' I decided to give him a test; I had time to kill. 'What's your favourite film?'

He really looked at a loss, as if he wasn't used to thinking about the positive things in his life. 'I don't know. I ... like old films. I ... yes, things like Humphrey Bogart, or courtroom dramas.' Spooky, I thought, is this Kismet? But films weren't what was on his mind. 'I was wondering ... I have some time before I start work. Would you like to come for a coffee?'

That needled me a bit, like he was doing me a favour. You know, penniless student taken under wing of older man, coffee and croissants and eternal gratitude. Been there, seen it, done it. And I don't wear the t-shirt. 'You don't do this often, do you?' I said.

He looked really hurt. 'Pardon?'

'Well, it's more polite to ask me for a coffee if *I* have time, not because *you* have.'

'I'm sorry – sorry, I know I shouldn't say that.' He blushed – he actually blushed – and I couldn't help liking him. 'I didn't mean that. I was trying to be polite. Casual. I don't have time really. I have to catch a bus in five minutes or I'll be half an hour late for my first class.' He shrugged.

'Would you like to come for a coffee anyway? If you have time?'

So I gave in: I've got a soft heart. 'I'm only teasing,' I said. 'A coffee would be nice.'

I led the way to the coffee shop. We went Dutch, honest, me with an espresso, him with a cappuccino. I perched myself on a stool in the corner by the window. I'd been here a few times before, when I'd missed my train home. It was okay, everything round, the tables, the stools, the brass pillars. He looked uncomfortable in his navy blue suit and burgundy tie. He wasn't losing his hair, but it stood up a bit at the back, too short. What I found myself thinking was, the opposite of round is square. Bitch, eh?

I could see him trying to wind himself up for what to say next: he was pretending to concentrate on inserting a spoonful of sugar into his cappuccino without disturbing the chocolate. He was like a surgeon. Then he decided.

'I like your hair,' he blurted.

Well, he looked as if he was about to panic and do a runner. 'Thanks,' I said. 'I'm auburn this month. A couple of months ago I tried to darken it. The roots were hellish to do.' I laughed. 'Vain besom, eh?'

'Not at all,' he said. God, he managed a smile back. 'I owe you an apology, about the paper. I read other people's papers on the train all the time. I've always wanted to say what you said. I was very rude.'

'And I shouldn't have been so pushy. Vain and pushy, that's me. And I steal my brother's chips.' I wasn't quite sure about him, not yet. Some guys are clear about what they're after right from the word go, but he didn't seem the type. Not that that's anything to go by. So I decided to give him some help. 'Okay. You're doing fine so far. Next part of the test. Do you cry?'

'Pardon?'

'Do you cry? You know, *A Star is Born*, *Casablanca*?' I winked: the whole situation got to my sense of the ridiculous. '*Brief Encounter*?'

'Well ... yes ... *Lassie Come Home*, when Bambi's mum dies, that sort of thing.'

I think he surprised himself by making me laugh. 'Good!' I said. 'That's lovely.'

'You're very good at this,' he said. 'Talking to people, I mean.'

'Well, everyone's got a story. Everyone's interesting, even just a wee bit. And what about you? You ask strange, pushy girls for coffee.'

'Oh no, this is a one-off,' he said, defensive like. 'I don't do this. I'm not too good at it. You might have noticed.'

'That's okay. But you must be good with people, standing up in front of all those students.'

He huffed. 'That's different. You play a part up there. Besides, most of my classes are apprentice plumbers. They're not exactly stimulating conversation.'

'What made you think I would be? Because I'm a girl?'

That threw him a bit, and I felt sort of sorry I'd said it. You can see most men walking a line, you know, between saying 'no, I'm a new man and can communicate with women as intellectual and social equals,' and 'yes, I am a red-blooded stud with a rod of iron down my trousers just for you, baby.' The trouble with him was I don't think he saw himself as either. And there was me putting him on the spot, the poor soul.

'No, not at all,' he said, too quickly. 'Well, maybe, a bit. I don't suppose I'd have asked you for a coffee if you'd been a man. But I probably wouldn't have asked a woman – not normally.'

'Don't you meet any stimulating women at work?'

'No, not really. Not on the staff.' He reddened a bit. 'The returning adults classes, there's a lot of women in them. They're nice, but they can be a bit ... forward, I suppose.'

'Not your type?'

He shook his head, looked slightly ashamed. 'No, but Anderson, a guy I work with, says they're sex-starved housewives who are gasping for it. Says there's plenty of fish in the sea and every session brings a new shoal. I don't really think that way, but ... '

'But sometimes you wonder?' He nodded, and I had to rescue him. 'Well, Anderson sounds like a bastard,' I said. 'It's okay to wonder, just as long as you're nice about it. Don't be a lech.'

He obviously felt a bit better. 'I don't think I ever could. I've always felt that ... you know ... teachers shouldn't, sort of, get involved. With students, I mean.'

'I wouldn't say they should never get involved,' I said, not wanting to call the kettle black, 'but you should be careful. You've got a lot of influence. Responsibility, I suppose. I mean, people's whole lives are affected by you. You're like doctors.'

'I don't think I've ever had a student I've affected that way. If I did, they didn't tell me.' And it really felt like it was a loss to him. 'Did you ever have a teacher like that?'

Yes, I did, but I didn't particularly want to talk about it. But he sat there, looking into his coffee, and it felt as if he would have waited forever for the answer.

'An Art teacher once. I wasn't that good, but he got me my results.' That didn't feel right, didn't really put it the right way. 'He said that it was important that I did it, that what I painted was mine. I nearly went to Art School because of him.'

'Why didn't you? You must have had some talent if he took an interest.'

'Things often don't work out,' I said.

'That's a pity. What happened?'

Sometimes you reach that point in a conversation when it all turns round just because of an innocent question and it becomes deep and important to you, even when you're talking to strangers, people you've just met at parties or in a cafe, when guards are down. And then only the truth will do, and it's not because you want them to know but because you want to know for yourself, to hear it said aloud to someone who doesn't even know your name. The gory truth.

'It's very personal,' I said.

'I'm sorry. I didn't mean to pry.'

'It's okay,' I said, and I had that feeling again that he'd sit there until I told him, not because he was pushy, just because he didn't know what else to do. And that was all right. I had to take a deep breath – me, smart arse – because I was finding it difficult to start. 'Well ... we went out together, me and my teacher, now and again, after I left school. I really liked him, his company. Sometimes I wondered if something could get going between us.'

'And it didn't?'

'No. It did. Once. We went to a concert. Prokofiev. Didn't do anything for me. Afterwards we went to his place for a drink. He told me how bad his life was. Declared undying love, but he really just wanted to fuck me. Sometimes men don't hear you when you're saying no politely.'

He was looking over my shoulder, up at the price list, the rows of coffee beans, anywhere but into my face. He looked like a wee boy who'd been caught out and wanted to be forgiven. 'Did he force you?'

'Depends what you mean. Men can get in your head sometimes when they want something. Then you see what they're really like. So I haven't painted for a while.' I stood up quickly, my knees trembling, and bent down to pick up my rucksack to cover it. 'I have to go now,' I said. 'I've already made you late for work. It was really nice meeting you.'

He got up half-way off his stool to stop me. 'Listen,' he said, 'what he did ... it's terrible. I mean ... the trust. Look, I'm thirty-seven years old. My name is William. People call me William. I ... I have a wife ... a boy of five ... we go to caravan parks for holidays. I take my son round museums of golf, for God's sake.' He held his hands out, not really knowing what to do with them. 'I'm not asking anything.

Really. I ... might have, earlier. I've never felt this inarticulate, not since ... can I see you again? Please?'

I wasn't even tempted, even though I believed him. Different worlds. Maybe he wanted to sample mine, bit more exciting than I reckoned his was. But you can go as far as you can with someone, sometimes too far, and then there's no point.

I held my hand out. He took it and we shook. 'I'm sorry,' I said. Me doing the apologising. 'You're a nice guy. Just keep it that way. Don't try to be anything different.'

And off I went. He saw me to the door of the shop, saying 'Goodbye,' and 'Thanks for your company,' really subdued and awkward. I wondered if he was watching me again as I crossed the station. Two newspaper vendors wolf-whistled me as I passed them. I felt sorry for having dumped all that on him – sorry for myself too – but I had to hurry to catch the train at eleven. I chanced a quick look back as I went through the barrier.

He was still there, but he was looking down at his feet, sort of puzzled by something, and all of a sudden, I swear, I knew he was wondering what the point was in spending so much of your life polishing a pair of shoes.

Twitchy

She didn't have much of a cleavage: I could see that when she bent low at the window. 'Ma name's Sandra,' she said, tits barely filling the wee white vest thing she had on underneath her tan suede jacket. She was classic: short black skirt, big heels, not stilettos though, those clumpy ones they sometimes wear. Bleached blonde, brown roots. Mascara smudged into the lines of the crow's feet at the edge of her eyes, lips thin like a slash, red lipstick smeared only on the centre, the fleshier bits. A real honey. Surely cheap.

'What'll twenty quid get me?' I asked. I wasn't bothered. I usually go to forty, but not for this slag.

'Whit? Twenty?' She laughed, more of a high whine. 'You'll be fuckin lucky tae get a fanny flash fur that. An ye'd huv tae pay fur the hotel room. Ur ye on the dole or whit? Ye skint?'

'I'm not paid 'til the end of the month,' I said. I could've managed, but I prefer them cheap. Nasty. No pretence. 'What about thirty?'

She blew out, straightened up, looked over towards the railings, deep into the bushes. Then she scanned the street, both ways. She hadn't had any takers. I could tell. She was cold. Needed money.

Why else?

'Ye cannae buy a hotel room?' I shook my head. 'Jesus, save me fae fuckin' skinflints.' She drummed her fingers on the roof of the car – my wife's, the old Metro – and spat her chewing gum into the gutter. 'Right. A hand job. In the car.'

'No,' I said. My wife has an acute sense of smell. 'We have to go somewhere.'

'Fuck's sake, you're a cheeky cunt. D'ye want fuckin jam on it?'

'If you're offering' I said. Not a bad idea.

'Eh?'

'Nothing,' I said. 'Do you want the business?'

She wasn't keen but she couldn't be fussy with a mug like that. The cold wind was blowing right through her, right through her whole life: you could see it, feel it.

'Ah've goat a friend, like. We can go tae his place. But Ah'll need an extra fiver fur him. Can ye dae that?'

I looked straight ahead. 'Yeah. If you strip while you do it. I want to feel you up while you do it.'

I almost lost her then. I'd rolled the window down and her hands were on the ledge. She leaned back, sort of growled and stomped her feet. But then she seemed to collapse inside. 'Christ pal, you're fuckin relentless,' she said, shaking her head. 'Blood fae a stone. Bastart.'

She wrenched the door open. Her heels clattered on the sill as she slid in. She turned, her knees pointing away from me, towards the door, as if she were keeping those thin, wasted legs to herself, refusing to let me look at them. Mean bitch.

We drove through the city centre, south along Eglinton. Her mate rented a place out there from a private landlord, a Paki. After that, she said nothing. When we arrived at this red-tiled detached house, it started to rain. The wipers swished up the screen, then juddered back dry with a sound like scraping furniture. 'You're lucky I came along,' I said. 'You'd be getting wet.'

'Gee fuckin ta,' she said, turned her face to the street. She could suit herself: I didn't pick her up for the conversation.

She had a key to get into the house. It was run down, with floors that sloped into the corners where the subsidence was worst, the kind of place that attracts dole merchants and FE students. There wasn't any sound of people, the clientele off to their usual Friday night entertainments, but in the huge kitchen off to the left, a dehumidifier roared away in the darkness. She led the way down a passage and a short flight of stairs towards the back to an interior door with a single Yale lock, then asked me for the thirty-five notes. She knocked, went straight in without waiting for a reply. 'Stay here,' she said, 'Ah'll be five minutes.'

I've never waited for a slag in my life. And I'd paid her. I stood there, my guts churning: I felt like punching her in the face for that. But I wanted to know what was in there, and I did something else I've never done. I went back out to the car, leaving the front door open so I didn't get locked out, and collected a couple of cans of Budweiser from the bag on the back seat, my Friday night. The idea of sharing a drink with a whore had never crossed my mind, not once in twelve years of using them. I stood outside the door, holding the cans together in one hand, gently clunking them together. The idea tickled me: bringing gifts, the perfect suitor.

The door opened and she looked at me standing there grinning, and then at the cans. A slight tut, a toss of the head aside, eyes cast. She stepped back to let me in. 'Meet Twitchy,' she said, turning away. 'This is Mr Tightarse. He's brought us a present.'

At first, I didn't register anyone else there. A wheelchair was parked in the corner of the room. I thought it contained a wax dummy of someone sculpted in the middle of an exhausted stretch, arms half raised above the head, legs held together, knees forced sideways. It didn't move, so I looked round the room. It was empty. I looked back, saw the same thing. But for the face. Eyes wide open, alert, jaw slung slack, glistening dribble.

'What's up with him?' I asked.

'Cerebral Palsy,' she said. I was surprised she could get her tongue round the syllables. 'He's no usually as bad as this. He's had a wee turn.' She stroked his head: it was shaved close, like a tennis ball.

'Does he live alone?'

'Naw. Well, sort of. His sister lives ower the road, in they tenements. She looks after 'im. But she works fae her hoose.'

'You'll need to give me her number.'

She snorted. 'Don't miss a fuckin chance, dae ye?' but I don't think she saw the ambiguity and I wasn't about to explain it. She began to wrap a red tartan rug around the guy's knees, tucking it under his calves and thighs. Then she stood up, moved behind the chair, flipped the brake off with the toe of her left shoe.

'What are you doing?'

'Whit the fuck dae ye think? Twitchy cannae exactly retire tae the smoking room, can he? Look around ye, fur Christ's sake. He'll wait ootside fur hauf an 'oor.'

It was a single room. One bed, covered in a washed-out beige candlewick bedspread. The lightshade was a small paper globe, dusty. One wardrobe, fifties, dark wood and burnished handles, scratched. An empty milk bottle, half a loaf of Sunblest and a black and white portable TV stood on a bare wallpaper-pasting table in the corner. A Calor gas heater, turned off, was shoved underneath it.

'Let him stay.'

'Whit? Ye cannae ...'

'Let him stay. It doesn't matter. It might make his Friday night.'

'Nae chance. You're fuckin sick. It isnae right.'

'Why not? You don't want him sitting out in the cold, do you? I'll give him ten quid. And he can have a beer as well.' I crossed the room, stood in front of him, looked down into his eyes, blue and wide: horrified, maybe. I prised open his fingers. They were solid and easily held the beer can. 'What do you say?' I asked him, and couldn't help laughing.

'You've got a choice,' I told her. 'Just get it over and done with, or I'll leave and find somebody else. But it's getting colder out there: won't be nice for you going back out in that.'

She looked at the man. 'Ah cannae,' she said. 'Ah promised his sister Ah wouldnae get him ... involved, like.' And then I had her: I knew she'd do anything to get out of it if I played my cards right. 'Please,' she said, 'Ah cannae.'

I pulled the ring on my beer can, just to point out I was staying, put it on the floor under the bed. 'Come here,' I said. 'I'll tell you what. You don't have to strip. You can keep your back to him: he won't see anything. It'll be done in a minute.'

And she came, meek as anything: they always do, they always have to. She leaned against me, unzipped my fly and began to work my cock. Quite well too, she got it up quickly. 'You're good,' I said. I put my fingers under her chin, tried to tilt her face up so that she could see my eyes – I've always liked that – but she jerked her head away. 'Look at me,' I said. She didn't, looked at my chest instead, just getting through. She was pushing her luck, I reckoned, so I wrapped my fingers in her hair and twisted her head up. 'Remember I'm paying you. I'm paying for your cooperation.'

It was simple to yank her onto her knees: it had to be done quick and hard, or I'd get a knee in the balls. Once they're down, they're fairly helpless: she reacted just as I thought, her hands coming up to her head, trying to ease my grip. She didn't think of hitting me. The guy came into view now, and all I could see were the whites of his eyes because his head was thrown back and he was looking down the length of his nose at the slag.

'Ye're no gettin that,' she said, practically whimpering. 'Ah'm no giein ye that.'

With my left hand, I reached into my jacket pocket, inside left breast. It struck me that, for a second, I got into a position that looked just like the guy, all contorted. But just for a second.

I flipped open my wallet, keeping hold of her hair, and got a fiver between my forefinger and thumb. I dangled it over the bed, so that the wallet fell, and reached down, waving the note in her face. 'That. On top of the thirty-five.' I shoved it down the front of her top: she jumped when my hand touched her tits.

So there we were: me holding this whore's hair

while she blows me off, and the cripple's sitting there, watching, and Christ knows what's going on in his head. I couldn't keep my eyes off him, and at first I thought nothing was in there, but then I noticed. It was the can of beer in his hand that gave the game away: it was twitching, slightly but really fast, and I noticed that he was doing it, that his whole body was shuddering, so quick that at a casual glance you'd think he was perfectly still. It was wild. I wondered if he was excited.

I was: it only took a minute, just like I'd promised her. When I came, I even closed my eyes. She gagged, drew her head back, coughed, gagged again and spat out between my feet: I kept my hand on her head, holding her down. 'Ur ye happy, ya fuckin shite,' she said, but quietly, sullen.

'Come on,' I said, 'it wasn't that bad. I haven't hurt you. Women like you get beaten up all the time.'

She drew me a look, really unpleasant. 'Ye goat whit ye wantit. Get yer hauns aff me. Get tae fuck.' I held my hand up, gestured out. She stood up, touched the guy's arm as she passed him, then went to the window to look out onto the street, just to get her back towards me.

I laughed. 'Please yourself,' I said, 'but I think you're being unreasonable. I've had a good time. I might have used you again. Regular customers must be like money in the bank.'

The guy made a noise, a sort of grunt. 'And what about you, Twitchy?' I asked. 'Have you had a good time?' I lifted my beer, tipped it in a matey 'cheers'. 'Of course you have. Haven't you?'

He sat there, warped, obscene. And he stared at me, stared and stared, and I realized I hadn't done up my fly, and he was staring at my cock, hanging out of my trousers. A weird rumbling started in his throat, catching on a breath in, building in intensity until there was no mistaking what was happening: he was laughing. At me. I was being laughed at by an idiot.

The whore just stood there: I wanted her to open

her slag mouth, I was daring her because then I could have kicked the shit out of something. But she was too smart for that. I looked at him, teeth full of black fillings and his eyes shining. How the fuck do you smash a spastic in the face? So I just had to get out. I unlatched the door – the beer can still in my hand – slammed it after me. I went up the stairs away from the room two at a time, but the runner must have been loose and worn because my foot caught in the top step. I went down hard, the can flying out of my hand, rattling and somersaulting along the hallway, rolling to a standstill against the front door. What was left of the beer gurgled onto the carpet.

I lay there for a second, watching the the puddle of foam spreading, the last of my carry-out. I'd paid forty quid for the privilege of being made to look an arsehole by a whore, a cretin and a fucking stair carpet. I wasn't having that. I picked myself up, rubbing my shin, dusted myself down. When I felt my jacket light, the pocket over my left breast empty, I remembered my wallet was still on the bed.

I stepped towards the room, and I heard the Yale lock snap. I thought about kicking it in, but the main door opened. Two girls came in, one saying 'Ooh, what's happened here,' as she squelched through the puddle of beer, then both looking at me, suspicious. They were quite tasty, but snooty, like university types, probably phone the police if I started anything. From inside, I could hear the guy laughing, on and on. I decided to leave it, turned down the hallway past the stuck-up kids. I half thought about chatting them up, see where I could get. But I had to hurry, because all the way out I could hear him braying, like a donkey at my back.

Drowning in the shallows

She's lying on top of me, kissing my neck, touching me softly, telling me I love you, Helen, and even through my jeans I can feel her, really close, and I can't help responding.

Shit fuck dammit.

She dumped me. This morning, I look in the bathroom mirror, see this zombie with bloodshot eyeballs staring back at me. I turn the cold tap on and plug the sink. My face feels overheated, raw, so I dip my head into the basin of water. I have to brush my teeth: usually do them before I go to bed, but last night I pass out in the middle of the third bottle of wine and fall asleep on the living room sofa. I wake up not knowing who I am, where I am, what happened. I reach out in panic for something – I have this drowning feeling – and pull over a small side table. What's left of a glass of wine seeps into the carpet. I remember then, feel worse.

Christ I'm going off my ...

The hallway floor is littered with compost and bits of ceramic. Her plant pot cops it with a hammer last night, stupid, *stupid*, and I trail her stuff all over the place trying to pack it into a cardboard box in the middle of the kitchen floor and my head feels like mince just now and I'm not up to stepping over it. I catch one flap of the top sticking up, stumble, crack my elbow off the edge of the washing machine, shit, shit, shit.

I look around at the mess I've caused and feel really fucking stupid, *stupid girl.* So what? She's left me. Everyone gets the elbow at least once in their lives, I tell myself, and I manage a smile because my elbow's still hurting like hell. Getting sozzled out of my box and wrecking the joint isn't going to do any good.

My cereal tastes like carpet underlay, but my stomach's empty after a day of no food and lots of drink, and I feel better now. I have a bath and tidy up. Cleaning the compost off the floor and hiding the box of her things where I can't see it are easy. Packing the last of her clothes isn't too clever, though, because I can smell her, her hair and her perfume, off her jackets and blouses and jumpers and every fucking thing, and I just push my face into the cloth and breathe deep and I'm almost off again, *stupid* cry-baby.

I need air. Get out. Go for a walk. I like Paisley in the summer, especially the Abbey, right next door to the town hall with its pillars like fat businessmen, but the Abbey's beautiful, mossy grey, quiet, cool. I buy a paper and two pints of milk and creep in to sit. Maybe I can think. Don't understand ...

Oh God

... don't understand the telephone call, but remember it all, every word. I see it coming, of course; if you want someone else, I tell her before she leaves, please say so and I'll know where I stand. No, she says, it's not going to happen, I love you more than anything, I always will, I could never be horrible to you. I look at her, her slimness, the way she stands there with her weight ever so slightly on one hip, and that lovely blonde bob bouncing like an advert as she shakes her head at the very idea. And the more she says it, the better I feel, I trust her, trust her, I do. Do I fuck.

'Hi, Helen, it's Julie,' she says.

'Hello, there,' I say, polite, polite, 'how are you? Are you having a good time?'

'Yeah, great. I'm rigging a sail like an expert.'

'That's good.' I take a breath, plunge in. 'How's Stuart?'

She sighs, annoyed. 'Stuart's fine. Why do you ask? It's obvious you don't like him.'

'I wouldn't say that,' I say, but I would, I don't, and then I break, snap so easy. 'It's just, like, I haven't seen much of you for two weeks now. I didn't think ... I didn't ... didn't ... you know, you've spent so much time with him.'

'So?'

'Nothing. You can do what you want, you've got the right to,' I say, but I'm lying, 'it's just ... I need to know ... I mean, why did you go away with him? I miss you.'

'I told you, didn't I? Lesley couldn't go. Christ, he's my oldest friend's husband. They've got three kids. Get off my back, you don't own me.'

And I feel she's going to hang up, and I say 'No, don't go, please!' stupid whining ...

And she stays and she takes a decision, just like that, on the phone, miles away from me where I can't see her or hold on to her. And I really want to hold her. 'Okay, Helen, what do you want to know? I won't lie to you, but you have to ask.'

Oh, clever, clever, my responsibility, my fault, and an audience shouts in my ear 'Open the box!' when I should take the money because this isn't a game show but I have to, have to see.

'Is he your lover?'

She's quiet for a moment. 'If you can call it that. I've fucked him. Once. Last night.' Casual.

And I feel as if I'm under glass, or water, and my vision of things is distorted. I can't say anything, but I open my mouth anyway and questions come spilling out, questions, questions.

'Did you enjoy it?' God why do I ask something as stupid as that, idiot, fool, stupid, *stupid girl*, Mum used to say, *always out of your depth.*

'No. Not particularly.'

'Are you going to do it again?'

'No. I don't know. He wants to. Perhaps.'

I'm crying by then, really bawling, and my voice is slurred and meaningless. When? How many times? Why? Are you coming back? What have I done wrong? Why?

And there's no chance of a conversation because I'm not making any sense and, sitting in the rear pews, I know that I've been all wrong, I've been obsessed when I should have been cool and logical and mature and understanding and she won't come back now.

A young minister, oily-haired and wearing Michael Caine specs, appears out of nowhere and lays a hand on my shoulder, awkward. 'Can I help you?' he asks. 'You seem upset.'

'No thanks,' I say, trying not to insult him by laughing. I want to scream in his face, shout that my girlfriend's left me because she's not all dyke and she's shagging her best friend's husband because no-one will suspect a thing, just to see his reaction, but I can't can't can't – 'I have to go.' I breeze past him, make sure I'm seen dropping a pound coin in the collection box.

I walk the mile or so home, past the Council HQ, its windows staring back at me, the police station, the leisure centre full of screaming kids, the tannery that smells of blood, the burnt-out night club where young guys used to fight each other at weekends, the playing fields where dogs go to crap. I stop at an off licence for another two bottles of wine.

When I get in, catch my breath, oh be still my beating heart, because the light on my answer machine's blinking and it takes a long while to rewind so it must be an important message and I'm sure I'm going to hear her voice, but it's only Gillian. She tells me I sounded drunk last night, but I don't remember phoning her, and she says she's sorry Julie's pissing me about but she's into control anyway and I should back off until things calm down; you've got time, she says, lots of time. She says her and Alec and the kids are going up to Orkney next week and they'd love me along, and she asks me if I remember the last holiday up there, and says 'love you, bye,' and hangs up.

Orkney, silly student thing when we were there before: get this insane urge to catch the mid-winter solstice at Maes Howe, but we spend our time taking speed and drinking Orkney whisky in Stromness and we get these blinding hangovers and miss the sunrise. So we race bikes – Gillian and Alec on their Suzukis, me on my brother's Kawa – along the Churchill barriers, scared stiff of dying amongst those concrete monoliths on the leeward side. The block ships fascinate me, all silted up. They look like newly hatched turtles heaving themselves out of the sand, and I think they must be really sad to find out they're already old and rusting and skeletal.

I say it's awful to use them like that, ripping their bellies out and sinking them just to protect new ships, after they've travelled all over the world, safeguarding men, building empires. I'm high-horsing it by then, getting emotional like I do sometimes after a trip, and say I'd like to see them put out to stud, or turned loose. Alec's dead practical, an engineer, calls me a romantic twit and says they're really useful because all the metal from World War I in them is uncontaminated by radiation, so scientists come back for samples, but I think that's worse, like cannibalism, and Gillian puts her arm round me and I cry softly for no reason.

Then the doorbell rings, and I'm feeling better, much more together thankyouverymuch, because I've decided to go to Orkney, but all that changes when I open the door and Julie's there and says 'Hi,' and kisses my cheek and comes in. I let her. She looks around, sees a picture is missing from the living room wall, one she bought me. She turns, tuts as if I'm a kid. 'You're not getting rid of me that easily,' she says, and she sets off on a search. The box isn't hard to find, and she begins to put everything back, 'just the way it was', and 'we'll put that back here, I never liked it over there anyway,' and she's indulgent and mature and she makes this low cooing sound when she says what we have is really special and I shouldn't be so silly. Everything feels so false, wrong, like she's playing a part, we both are, being civilized in this shitty scene, and I feel like screaming – SCREAMING – but I want her to stay, please stay, so I follow her around my home.

'I have to ask this,' she says, serious. 'It wasn't Stuart's fault. I came on to him, Helen. You're not going to hurt him, are you?'

'No,' I say, and wonder why, why not fuck him right up, poor wife and kids, and what about Me ...

'Good. I told him you wouldn't feel like that.' She stops, takes my hand. 'I've missed you. I was worried, so I came down for the afternoon. I'll need to get back to the boat tonight – I'm learning "Navigation in the Dark", or something like that.' She laughs, that husky laugh that's full of lust, but I wonder why the whole thing feels so stilted. 'Come and give me a cuddle.'

I'm led to my living room, and she holds me gently for a while. We stretch out and she lies beside me, her head on my shoulder. She breathes in my ear, kisses the back of my neck, winds her leg around mine, pushing herself against my thigh. 'I love you, Helen,' she whispers, and she takes my hand and places it on her breast

don't let her do this,
don't let her
stupid girl, Mum would say
getting out of your depth again

and she's wearing a thin floral dress and she hasn't got a bra on and I can feel her under my fingers even though I'm really half-hearted. For ages and ages I lie there and feel as if there's something slithering about in the pit of my stomach, but she's concentrating too much on getting to her own orgasm to notice.

She brightens after she's finished, ruffles my hair. 'Come on, honey, don't be so glum.' She pouts at me, giggles. 'Okay, things have changed, but it's not a disaster. You're still my best friend. We can still be friends, can't we?'

'I don't know. I can't say just now.'

'Easy', she says, 'I'll say it for you. I've never been closer to anyone. So. Friends?'

'I want more than friends.' Little girl, want, want, want. 'Especially now.'

She sits up, astride my hips, hitching her dress up slightly, and oh God I can feel her heat. She leans towards my face, clear, clear blue eyes. She smiles, knowing.

'Well', she says, 'we can still play. Let's face it, you do things for me Stuart can't.' She bends down to brush her nose against mine for a second. 'Mmm. Friends who smooch and have orgasms, eh?'

It sounds such a daft phrase, artificial, something in the script, like nothing she's ever said before. Then I realise she's brought it straight from the bed she's fucked him in and it's still warm, still warm from the fucking.

Something happens, deep inside me, like a bomb going off, and I tilt and lurch, and I've got that feeling again of being submerged, of me sinking through the back of my head.

And she's lying on top of me, kissing my neck, touching me softly, telling me I love you, Helen, and even through my jeans I can feel her, really close, and I can't help responding.

Newton's cradle

You know what a Newton's Cradle is? Used to be a big thing with aspiring young couples in the seventies, along with wave machines, or lava lamps – now they were *really* trendy. It's a line of chrome balls suspended in a frame. You lift a ball at one end, let it go and it swings down, sending the one at the other end flying up, with the ones in the middle staying still. Well, that's what my marriage was like before we jacked it in and got divorced: me at one end, my wife at the other, the baggage of fifteen years stationary in the middle but essential to the dynamics of it all. What I recollect most about the situation at the time, though, were the moments of collision: really interesting things could happen then.

Funnily enough, we often ended up screwing the arse off each other, really wild sex that'd never been better, even though we loathed each other. My wife had a boyfriend, some whey-faced cunt from her work who shat himself every time he saw me; and I was living with a doctor, Penny, at the time. I've never bothered much about fidelity: a string of places to bolt to is useful sometimes, and women'll always accommodate a misunderstood soul.

Other times, the venom would surface. She'd claw, scratch, throw things at me; occasionally I'd give her the back of my fist across her mouth, nothing that would mark her too much. I never touched my son, though, he was okay: hard and muscular, but easy going. He inherited my quickness, the sharpness of wit that keeps you ahead of the dromedaries in life. Besides, I didn't want to antagonize him too much: at fourteen, he was already taller than me. I recognized future bruising there.

There was one occasion we were in some bar, 'talking it over' she called it. Sex wasn't on the agenda: she was too angry because I was refusing to pay the mortgage again. And it wasn't a particularly romantic setting. The bar was done out in red leatherette and dark brown formica, the stuff that was supposed to look like wood. The carpet had been red too, once, but was stained with beer and threadbare from heavy working boots. The ceiling was covered in the type of nicotine-encrusted Artex that resembles solid ochre custard. I picked places like this deliberately: they allowed me to choose to stand between her and the gawping of the punters who'd never seen anything like her before. If I felt like it. And if she refused to go in, she had no chance of keeping the house: she hadn't yet discovered the joys of the court order.

I remember there were two young guys at the fruit machine: one in black leather, cropped blond hair, the other shorter and more furtive, dark-haired, square jawed. They looked over now and again, appraising my wife. I noticed a couple of surreptitious gestures which remarked on her breasts, some hand movements which indicated how much they'd like to fuck her. She saw it too, and I knew she'd be furious. I enjoyed that.

There was one other customer, an old man in a brown anorak and grey trousers held up by a cheap plastic belt. He was obviously a local: the barman had automatically served him with the correct brand of whisky when he'd entered, but had studiously ignored him afterwards, finding glasses to wipe and gantries to polish. The old man simply nursed his drink in silence, lowering and twisting his head towards us occasionally, his tongue flickering across his lips as if tasting the tension from the far corner where we sat.

But he was drunk and impatient for an audience, and he preferred the look of us to the gamblers. When he was halfway across the floor and it was obvious we were his target, my wife lowered her head, muttering 'Shit' into her lap. He was about sixty, short, white-haired, his left cheek bone horse-shod by a tumbler-sized scar. He stopped in front of us, his whisky glass in his left hand, his right rubbing his scrubby chin thoughtfully, like a zoologist discovering a brand new species in his own back garden.

'How ye daein?' he asked. The wife's 'Fine' was as

cold as she could muster, but I nodded, beckoned him to sit at our table. I could feel a game approaching.

'Huvny seen ye in here afore,' he said. 'No exactly your kinda place, is it?'

I gave him some crap about the beer being good, about me coming in here years ago when I worked up in the shipyards. I could tell he didn't believe me, that I was bullshitting him, but he was prepared to go along with it for now.

'Yer lassie disnae exactly fit in, dis she?'

That was all right: guys in pubs often wonder what she's doing with me, until they get talking to me. But it didn't suit her.

'I'm his wife, actually, not his "lassie",' she said. 'And we're trying to have a private talk and a quiet drink. Would you leave us alone?'

He just looked at her, as if he didn't understand, but he did, I could tell. 'Aw come oan, hen, Ah'm jist lookin furra bit o company. Ye can spare an auld man a wee while, can't ye? Ah'll no hurt ye.'

I was amazed he was still sober enough to be patronizing. I knew the wife wanted me to back her up, ask him to leave, but I was having a great time and I wasn't letting the momentum go, not just yet. I asked him what his trade was, expecting him to be a retired welder or something like that.

'Ah'm a writer,' he said. I suppose some surprise must have registered, because he straightened up and stared into my face. 'Aye, Ah am. Widnae know, wid ye? Think Ah'm jist a tosspot, eh?'

Yeah, I thought, that's a good enough description. But he was a writer. He fished out a book of poetry from deep inside his coat, some dog-eared local pamphlet from way back, and there was a whole section of his stuff, complete with a picture of him on the front looking twenty years younger, all moody and self-important. 'Potentially a major contemporary talent', the blurb said. He didn't look contemporary now.

I offered it to my wife: 'We don't really have time for this,' she said, but I said a few minutes wouldn't hurt, and I held it there, in front of her, until she couldn't decline any longer without antagonizing the man. He turned to me only when she opened the book and began to read the dozen or so poems he had written.

'No bad, eh?' he said to me. 'Long time ago, mind ye. Aye, a fuckin lifetime ago, Ah'll tell ye. Nae bloody use, they bastarts that ur in noo,' he grumbled. 'Ah wisnae part o their arse-lickin' set, that wis ma problem. Bastarts. Bastarts.'

He went on, and I joined in, slagging off one writer I enjoyed reading or another I'd never heard of. I bought him a couple of drinks – during my visits to the bar, he never spoke to the wife, simply stared at her while she kept her head down, pretending to read – and he got more and more matey, thinking he'd found a mug.

Eventually, the wife couldn't stand it any longer. She wanted out of it as soon as possible – I could feel it in her – but she wasn't going to get the message across by ignoring us. She closed the book and placed it on the table. She leaned against me, her mouth close to my ear. 'Can we leave now?'

'So, whit dae ye think, hen?' he asked. 'Ur ye impressed?'

She didn't want to speak to him, but I just raised my eyebrows, giving her no option but to reply to him. 'I think they're very good,' she said.

Bad move, I thought, and I was right. He leaned forward, across the table at her. 'Ye reckon? An whit dae YOU know?'

She was confused, set back, had been sure one of her condescending compliments was required. 'I'm ... I suppose ...' she floundered, and then hung herself. 'Well ... I'm an English teacher.'

'Oh, ur ye?' He hissed like a firework. 'Ah don't gie a toss. Ah fuckin hate English teachers. They used tae belt me fur ma spellin. Ah went tae wan o they writers' groups wance until some o you fuckin wankers turned up. Fuckin killt it, whinin oan aboot split infinitives and the use o the fuckin colon.' He jabbed his finger at her and I felt her flinch. 'Colons, darlin, belong up arses.'

I loved that: the guy was quick. The wife was livid, turned to gather her coat and handbag, said 'I don't have to take this from an old piss artist like him, even if you won't do anything about it.' I stood up, told her it was okay, that I was just going to the toilet and we hadn't sorted out the mortgage yet and she just about died. Then he said, 'Ah think Ah'll join ye, son,' and I saw her relief.

The toilet stank, the brown-tiled floor awash with paddled piss and cigarette ends. I stepped over a long slug trail of sodden toilet paper to reach the urinal, its drain choked with debris. I was determined to finish as quickly as I could: the stench was unbearable.

Beside me, the old writer leaned on stretched arms against the wall, staring down at his feet, puffing heavily. He didn't seem to need to go any longer, but he cleared his throat several times, spitting out the phlegm, and looked down, between my legs, now and again. He chose his moment, speaking just as I finished and was shaking my prick dry. 'Dae ye fancy goin intae a cubicle, son?' He slurred his speech so much the meaning of what he said was almost lost. I stopped, thought for a second, zipped up my trousers and turned towards him.

'Like, ye're no exactly happy wi her, ur ye? I mean, whit's a blow job? Disnae mean wur bent. Ah'll dae it fur a fiver.' He was suddenly very lucid, the fog clearing from his eyes. 'An ye go oot there an ye look at each other an ye know sumthin she disnae. Exclusion, son. That's excitement. That's power.'

I don't know what I felt, something strange, something ... it doesn't matter, but I remember being surprised by my own erection. So I stepped back from him. I reached into my jacket pocket and fished out a handful of change – just dross – and extended my hand outwards straight. The old guy looked at me as if I was going to be crucified. I dropped the coins into the urinal, one by one, hearing each soft, chinking little plop. He seemed fascinated, so I watched the last one, a twopence piece, pirouette in the air and into the trough to join the others. They lay there, and they were amazing, transformed, glittering like doubloons in the stagnant urine.

And what did the drunken old bastard do? I watched him, awestruck. I noticed the tiny gathering of spittle at the corners of his mouth, and his pock-marked eyeballs, like warts, and his pitted nose, as he carefully rolled up his sleeve and bent over to retrieve the coins.

Without thinking and with one swing of my leg, I whipped the feet from under him. There was nothing personal: it was just a reaction, any reaction would have done. He fell forward, his face thudding against the porcelain. I heard his nose break, the cartilaginous crack loud in the silence. He slid down into the piss, face first, and lay there for a moment before levering himself up onto his knees. I looked at him, soaked from head to waist, and I felt incredibly heady. He would go out into the bar and everyone would see just what he was, and I revelled in that. The sensation was so powerful I had to lean against the wall to steady myself before I left him there, whimpering and snorting blood and mucus through his fingers.

In the bar, the blond thug from the slot machine had moved in and was leaning over my wife, showing her a tattoo on his upper arm, leering down her cleavage. She threw a wild look at me, full of reproach, promising me that by God I'd pay for this. I didn't care. I was on a high, the adrenalin propelling me right past her and out into the street, almost hearing the air rush past my ear on the way. I think I smiled.

Unto myself

Everyone on the island guessed that Julia MacDonald killed her husband, but only Father Joseph and the old woman ever knew for certain.

The priest answered the door of his cottage at one in the morning of a stormy Thursday, eight months ago now, and peered blearily into the lashing rain at the wild beauty who twisted and wrung herself on his doorstep. Her dress was black with rain and blood.

'Oh God, come in child,' he'd said, vaguely uneasy at the cliché. Nothing else came to mind, though. She leaped inside: he led her to a chair by the hearth. The fire had long since gone out. Such a lot to think about. Light the stove and put the kettle on. Collect a pail of peat. Warm the teapot. Build up the fire. Two spoons and one for the pot. Light the kindling.

Check that the blood soaking her dress wasn't hers.

Later, he wondered why he thought of that last, but perhaps he knew the instant he opened the door and saw her standing there that she'd killed her husband. Perhaps he knew that, if the blood was hers, it would have been Ewan to blame for it, and he would not have left her upright.

He bent at the fire, listening to her rasping breath catching in and out, hearing the china cup rattle in its saucer. She didn't drink her tea, and when he turned towards her after the orange sputters could survive untended, it was cooling – white borders around a caramel-coloured scum. Her head was hung, her hair wet, straggling over her eyes and the blue towel he had wrapped around her shoulders.

'Now, Julia, what's happened?'

She twisted her head from side to side, as if to dislodge a thought from her mind so that she might be able to speak it and then disown it.

'Julia. Listen to me. Whatever it is you have to tell me, it must be said. If it's to be made better, it *must* be said.

Do you understand? Julia?'

She nodded, fiercely and with a spirit that made him sick with fear for her. 'I've done a terrible thing. I didn't know where to go. I'm so sorry.'

'What is it, Julia?'

'Ewan's dead. I've murdered him. I didn't mean to.'

'Tell me what happened, Julia.'

'He came back from Sandy's, drunk on the whisky. He'd been arguing with them. He told them he'd been taking eggs from the west cliffs, from down in the gully. They said it couldn't be done, called him a braggart. He was going to go, then and there, Father, raid the nesting ledges in the gully. He'd told them he would show them. I tried to stop him, Father. He would have killed himself ... '

Her eyes filled again and her hands flew to her mouth to smother the horror of her irony. She looked up at him as if she were at the bottom of a well.

'I held on to him. His arm. He told me to leave him be, that he was sick of me and my ugly face. He went out the door. I was still holding him, telling him not to be so stupid, going there when he was drunk. He hit me then.' She touched her cheekbone: a grey-bluish bruise was beginning to appear. 'I just held on, Father. I didn't want him to go, not in that condition, and in this weather. He had his knife. He said I was just scared, a stupid, frightened rabbit and he was going to skin me like one. I thought he was going to do it, Father, I really did.'

'I know, I know, Julia. We *all* know how Ewan treats you.'

'I was struggling with him. He was very drunk, but very strong. The knife fell and I picked it up but he called me a bitch and worse, so much worse, and I thought he was going to kill me and I hit him and hit him and when I looked I had the knife in my hand.'

She was spent, and fell silent. The clock ticked on and Father Joseph thought and thought and thought, all for the benefit of the young woman. He had watched her grow up, a tiny smudge of a girl all swirling hair and impetuous grins who had learned to read and write at an earlier age than anyone else on the island, as far back as they could remember. She had so much promise, perhaps even university on the mainland and a career as a doctor. Then Ewan MacDonald, her second cousin – five years her senior and educated in brutality by a father who came home from the Great War shell-shocked and widowed during his absence – married her.

There were two ways of wooing on the island: the first entailed sheepish glances, giggling, nervous thrustings of sparse flowers or bags of toffee; Ewan's was the other way. He simply claimed her as his possession. Before her eighteenth birthday, she lost a son in her womb: she'd slipped on an icy step, she said, though the women gossiped that the mark on her belly looked like a fist. She lurched into hounded silence after that. If she had a brain, she never allowed herself to show it, and her face collapsed into despair. His heart had ached for the lassie.

Twenty-five years he'd cared for these people, discounting his time in the War: they left, came back, left for good. The island was dying. Four young men were to move to the mainland ports to work the big trawlers, and their families would go with them and the community would wither. Ewan MacDonald had spoken of it too. Already men from the authorities had held meetings in the chapel, explaining to the islanders the unsustainabilty of their community, how the lives they led would no longer be viable.

What good would it do, to hang this lassie, when everyone who could remember Ewan MacDonald would soon be scattered across the world?

'Julia. Listen to me. You are right. You didn't mean it. You were defending yourself. Therefore *it is not* murder. And no-one will judge you, except perhaps God. But you must do what I say.'

'I killed him, Father. That is what they'll say, and they are right.'

'They will only say that if they know, Julia. Only if

they know.'

And he led her. She had come over the hill, not by the shore past the cottages. No-one would have seen her. So he fetched the little pony from the byre abutting the cottage and they set off, back over the hill, leaning into the wind, both wrapped in his coats and his scarves and his gloves, the little paraffin lamp's shields directing a beam ahead. They arrived at MacDonald's croft before three. From half a mile away he saw the front door still lying open: a lozenge of watery yellow light threw itself over the doorstep, and he was strangely appalled by it.

Ewan lay thirty feet from the doorway. The grass around him was soaked with blood, but it would seep into the ground, wash away. He would be dammed for it, but found himself thanking God that it had not happened inside, where there would be blood on the carpet and furniture.

Julia silently did as she was told: she helped him haul the body of her husband over the little pony; she fetched half a dozen buckets of water to rinse the ground where he had died; she went inside and washed and changed into a clean dress; she bundled up her blood-soaked dress and underclothes and handed them meekly to the priest, along with his coat. And all the time, he held his breath, waiting for her to snap like a twig.

'Now listen to me, Julia. In the morning, you must go to Donald by the shore. Tell him everything up to the point when Ewan came home. You were asleep and you heard him come in. He was very drunk. You rolled over to go back to sleep, expecting him to come to bed. In the morning, he wasn't there, and you are reporting him missing. Do you understand?'

She nodded, but he was sure that she most certainly did not understand.

'Julia. Ewan was a man, and so deserves to be mourned as a man. But he was one of the blackest souls I have ever known. No-one on the island had a good word for him, other than his grandmother, though God forgive us for being silent on his mistreatment of you. And no-one, especially me, will allow you to be tortured for his death at the fault of his own violence. *Especially* me, Julia. Do you hear me?'

The girl jerked away from his hands on her shoulders. 'Is it not wrong, Father? It must be wrong.'

'You let me worry about that, Julia. I will take care of your guilt. I absolve you now and, whatever happens after this moment, I will take the blame myself. You must live on, Julia. You are a young woman. You *must* live on.'

She shook her head and, for a moment, he thought he had lost her. But she drew herself up. 'What will you do with him?'

'You let me take care of that. It's better that you don't know.' She looked pained, and he added, 'I will bury him carefully. He will be in hallowed ground. I promise.'

She nodded, just once, said 'Thank you, Father,' very softly and went inside. The door closed and he was left with Ewan MacDonald.

He had to hurry: it was almost four, and he had much to do. The little pony struggled under the dead weight, back over the hill. The priest unlashed Ewan's corpse and dragged it into the cleit on the slope of the hill above his cottage. He searched and emptied the dead man's jacket pockets, then scrabbled peat over the body until it was covered. He would deal with it more permanently later. He had to get over to the west cliffs, so he mounted the old pony again and set off.

The grey horizon was softening by the time he got there; perhaps it was just as well, no-one could approach the cliffs easily in the dark. They slashed deep inland, and forty years earlier MacDonald of the hill had fallen down a ravine and broken his neck when he was still half a mile from the sea.

He knew the gully Julia spoke of: two hundred and fifty feet of sheer black basalt that only razorbills and fulmars clung to, their feet slipping and sliding, their eggs rolling about and their chicks huddling and shaking. No-one climbed there. The old ones had said it was an evil place, but most of them were dead now.

Tethering the pony to a rock, he hunkered down and slid to the edge. Edges were everywhere on the island, upward grassy slopes that tempted a walking man on and on until one further astonished step ended in a tumble through clean air onto the rocks below. The surge sucked at the gully, foam racing down towards the sea and away. Anything falling into that could be dragged out, carried off on currents that had deposited cows in Norway, it was said. That's what they had to think. He took Ewan's cigarettes and petrol lighter and left them as near the edge as he dared. Then he flung a shoe, as hard as he could, over the rim.

It was seven by the time he got home, but no-one would have been around: they let him sleep most mornings; the Stewart girl was meant to come at eight to serve him his breakfast, though she rarely arrived before a quarter past. He would have time to wash, shave and put on the disguise of a fresh morning face.

ii

The investigations were straightforward. Donald of the shore, in his capacity as island constable, interviewed those who had spent the evening with Ewan. He said nothing about the fact that they had all been drunk on the produce of Sandy's still: after all, Donald was only called on to be a constable one or two days a year, and enjoyed the illicit whisky himself on any one of the other three hundred and sixty-three that took his fancy. Yes, they agreed, Ewan had been very, very drunk and perhaps they shouldn't have made fun of him when he told them of his exploits at the west cliffs, but they couldn't resist: after all, they outnumbered him and he wasn't steady enough on his feet to fight them. How was Julia? they wanted to know. Did Ewan tell her where he was going? Had Donald tried the west cliffs?

At the gully, Donald found Ewan's lighter and

cigarettes. He could see nothing from the cliff edge, so tramped back and commandeered old Alec's services and dinghy. They puttered up the gully – itself quite a dangerous manoeuvre – and Donald scanned the base of the cliffs with his binoculars. He spotted a single shoe, wedged in a crack filled with seaweed.

He called on the priest. He stood in Father Joseph's parlour, his bigness filling the room. His hands were behind his back and he rocked, ever so lightly, on the balls of his feet, as if this posture compensated for his lack of an official uniform. A brown-paper bag containing Ewan's lighter and cigarettes was handed over, and Donald, red-faced, quietly begged his pardon and asked if he could possibly; 'I'm no good at this, Father, you know ... '

Of course, said Father Joseph, I'll tell her, and Donald had shuffled even more nervously and mentioned the mark on Julia's face. Father Joseph could see the big man's mind lumbering inside an unfamiliar logic. If Ewan had hit her, she would have spoken to him, and would have known where he was going. Why didn't she stop him? Why didn't she fetch help at the time? Why hadn't she said where he was going when she reported him missing?

'Don't trouble yourself about it, Donald. Julia was rarely without a mark from the man's hand. He could have done it before he went to Sandy's.'

The constable's face softened: he wasn't a stupid man, but he was compassionate and more likely to think the best of folk. 'Aye, Father, I'm sure you're right. If you could inform her of her husband's death then. In the meantime, I'll organise Alec to search for the body, though it'll have been carried off by now, no doubt.'

Father Joseph walked over to Julia's, clutching his hat to his head: the pony was tired and needed rest, so he left it grazing on the hill. He went round by the shore, past the cottages, and women stood in their doorways, watching him with a curiosity that would have been insolent if he had not buried their fathers and husbands.

'Is it true Ewan MacDonald's fallen down the gully and killed himself?' asked Shona, the wife of Duncan the boat mender. She was a kind young woman, had lost bairns in her womb four times now. Duncan wanted to move to the mainland, was sure Shona could be looked after better there, and he could have the son and daughter he craved.

'Well, Shona', he replied, 'we'll have to see.'

'God forgive me for saying it, but she'll be a might happier if he has.'

The priest smiled wanly, hoping to communicate disapproval but some measure of agreement. 'Besides, there's a wife waiting to know what's happened. She must be first.'

'Aye. I wonder if old Mrs MacDonald would see it that way though.'

'Donald will be the one to tell *her*, Shona. She's not one of my parishioners and I doubt if she'd welcome me with the news.' He hurried on, the last few syllables said over his shoulder, urgently though not impolitely.

Men were down at the shore, loading their boats for fishing. They were afraid of death because they lived with it much more immediately and regularly than their women, so they turned their backs, as mannerly and respectfully as they could. One of their own had been taken, even if they had no love for him.

Julia jumped when she opened the door, then sighed and wilted into a chair. He made her a lunch of soda bread and herring, scattered grain for the chickens, washed her dishes and tidied her kitchen, all the time soothing her, don't worry girl, it is all right, try to put any other version of what happened out of your mind. By mid afternoon, he was finished, and he left her blank and vacant but, he felt sure, strong enough to say nothing.

At the end of the path, the women had gathered, baskets covered and mourning shawls on. He often marvelled at the haste of Catholic women to mourn collectively, had seen it in Ireland and Italy and here from his very first days. He knew better than to deny the urge.

'Can we see her now, Father?' asked Shona.

'Well, she's eaten and is feeling better. I think she's in deep shock now, so go carefully and quietly. She has wept enough and I think she needs healing time and simple support.'

They scuttered off up the lane and past him, perhaps peeved at his lecture on the etiquette of bereavement. Still, Julia would have to face the womenfolk sometime. Including Ewan's grandmother.

iii

A mass was held for Ewan on the Sunday, memorial in all but name. Father Joseph spoke of God's mercy and the gift of everlasting life, and of Jonah and the Whale and how it was to be hoped that the sea would give back to them what it had taken. He did not openly discount the possibility of the miracle of Ewan being found alive, but neither did he encourage false hopes. They sang psalms traditional and appropriate, and everyone seemed at ease.

He'd buried Ewan the previous night. He'd gone to bed early to catch up on sleep, and left the chimes on the clock. He'd risen at two, had a cup of strong, sweet tea, put on his oldest clothes, gone to the cleit, dismantled the pile of peat and exhumed Ewan MacDonald.

The body was still remarkably fresh, though stiff, and he felt something of the waste of the man, of his life as well as his death. Then he dug a hole deep enough, said prayers over Ewan, absolved him, blessed the ground with holy water and tipped him in.

He was used to treating corpses nonchalantly. He'd lied about his age, knocked ten years off, to chaplain a regiment during the Great War, and became accustomed to distinguishing between the souls of boys and the withered, blackened stumps of flesh they left on earth. The Somme had taught him that respect for dead meat was a luxury. So he hopped and stepped and jumped on the soil to level it and, had any of his parishioners sneaked in to watch from the little low door of the cleit, they would have suspected him of jigging with the de'il.

He managed it all remarkably quickly, piling up the peat over the grave and scattering the excess soil over the mound, and he'd managed a good wash and back to bed so that the congregation saw no darkness in either his fingernails or under his eyes when he shook hands with each of them at the chapel door. Julia was supported by her family, a mother and brothers and sisters, as insubstantial as charcoal line drawings in the stoor of the morning. They each shook his hand, thanked him kindly for all he had done, so much more than anyone could have expected. Then the whole congregation shuffled down the pebbly path.

A third of the way to the village, they were met by a black creature. It stood slightly to the left of the congregation's path, gripping the stane dyke of a madly ungeometric sheep fank, but there was no doubting that old Mrs MacDonald was here to halt the procession. Father Joseph pushed himself to the front of the little knot of folk and stepped over the grass towards her.

'Mrs MacDonald. My condolences. We will all miss your grandson.'

In her leathered, lined face he saw nothing he could recognize as humanity or compassion or suffering. She stared fiercely, with the sure knowledge that Father Joseph had been damned the day he was born.

'Keep your hypocrisy and your pious sympathies, man. And rest assured that whatever pleas to your god you said in yon degenerate place you call a church went unheeded, and better is my grandson for it.'

'Please, Mrs MacDonald, this is a time for us to mourn together, to gain strength from each other.'

'I have no need of the strength you offer.' Her eyes

scanned over his shoulder and pierced Julia. 'Aye. There's the hoor. There's the murderess.'

'Mrs MacDonald, there's no need for that. What happened to Ewan was an accident, a terrible accident.'

'No it wasn't. I saw. I *saw*. As clear as day it came to me, her hitting my grandson and her hands slicing into his very heart. You all know me. You know I have the sight.'

There was muttering behind him: yes, the old witch had that reputation, had foreseen the squall that took Angus and his son. She was the last to have the sight, the wireless being more reliable in the 1930s.

'Forgive me for being so blunt, Mrs MacDonald, but no-one was to blame except Ewan himself. It happened as a result of his own foolishness: let's not make matters worse with even more foolishness like this.'

He doubted if anyone had ever spoken to her like that since 1905, when she was midwife and McAlpine the missionary had come to the island and fought long and hard with her. She had attended the women in labour, sealed the umbilicus in the old way with a mixture of seabird oil and dung. McAlpine had heard of St Kilda, of the work of Fiddes, and arrived with antiseptics and strange new-fangled terms like '*tetanus infantus*' so the old woman had found herself reviled and blamed for generations of lost bairns buried within a week of being brought into the world. And she had retreated steadily into her bitter paganism. Everyone feared and avoided her.

'Don't get above yourself,' she said. 'Remember that you are only a man.'

He stood his ground, meeting her eye. She could only be ten years or so older than he was, yet she seemed timeless, a granite Medusa. She turned, a look of the righteousness and the distaste with which she must have dismissed the missionary all those years ago smirking around her mouth, and strode off down the hill, seeming huge despite her bowed back.

He sighed and waited until she was well out of

harm's way before he clapped his hands together and swung round. 'Well, now, that was unpleasant, but Mrs MacDonald is old and I suppose we have to make ...'

But no-one was looking at him. All the faces wore worried expressions, doubting eyes under shawls and caps, as they regarded Julia. She had whitened and shivered, her dark eyes beneath her dark hair seeming hunted and terrified.

It was, without a doubt, a face full of guilt.

iv

Donald sent word of the death on the first boat out, and three weeks after Ewan's disappearance the police from the mainland arrived to put their seal of approval on it all. The two policemen who came were detectives, a strange breed of supermen read about in the occasional novel which found its way to the island. They were taller than the island men, and wore long tweed coats and felt hats, and polished brogues at which they tutted frequently, collecting mud and clay and dung wherever they trod.

Donald and Father Joseph conducted them around the island. He interviewed Sandy's and Ewan's other drinking cronies: they were suitably sullen and suspicious, and the whisky they drank on the fatal night had been brought on the Christmas boat last year, oh yes, they'd been saving it special. The detectives asked Shona and two other women about the relationship between Ewan and Julia, as if they would tell them even though they knew, and they scowled and said much the same as anyone else. They saw Julia, poor sweet lost Julia. They must have felt they were whispering down a long tunnel at a frightened creature trapped underground. But she answered their questions eventually, managing little more than yes or no. She's taken it hard, said Murdoch, a ginger-haired youth who thought that the womenfolk had a fancy for him given the way their eyes followed him, though in truth they were simply astonished at the hairlessness of his chin.

They spoke of it all being open and shut, of how accidents happened when drink was involved, and the older of the men, Forbes, a scrub-jawed angular city man, complimented Donald for his paperwork as they waited on the jetty for the boat to putter alongside. They were shaking hands when Murdoch looked over Father Joseph's shoulder, back along the jetty, and said, 'Hello, who's this?'

Mrs MacDonald came tap-tap-tapping along the planking, brandishing the walking stick she'd taken to. 'Are you the policemen from the mainland?' she called.

The two detectives looked at each other. 'What did she say?' asked Murdoch.

Donald looked grey and sick. 'It's Mrs MacDonald,' he said. 'She doesn't have the English.'

The old woman eased Donald aside and stood under Forbes' nose. 'Ask them if they've found my grandson,' she said over her shoulder.

'She's wondering if you've found Ewan's body.'

Forbes shook his head and raised his voice. 'No, Mrs MacDonald, I'm afraid not. We don't know when it'll be found.'

'Tell the Protestant fool I'm not deaf or wandered. Have you told him Julia killed Ewan?'

Donald's mouth opened and stayed that way, though the only sound he could make was a gurgling at the back of his throat. Father Joseph stepped forward.

'Gentlemen, Mrs MacDonald says Ewan was murdered by his wife.'

Father Joseph was amazed by the way the men stiffened without actually moving, as if they'd been trained to show emotion in the most emotionless manner possible. It was Forbes who spoke, though Father Joseph suspected that Murdoch was the more excited, perhaps a young man with an eye to promotion.

'Really, Father. Could you ask her how she

knows this?'

'I don't need to. Everyone on the island knows. She saw it.'

Murdoch could no longer contain himself. 'She saw it? You mean she's a witness to a murder? Why didn't you tell us about this?'

Donald looked as if he were afloat, out of control on a rough sea. 'Well ...' he said, but nothing came, and he raised his arms by his side in a gesture of absolute ambiguity.

'Well, no, she's not quite what you would call an actual witness,' said Father Joseph. 'Mrs MacDonald saw it in a vision.'

'What?'

'A vision, Inspector Forbes. Mrs MacDonald has what is called the sight.'

Forbes looked at his junior's crestfallen face and smiled. 'Never mind, Murdoch, your hour'll come.' He looked at Mrs MacDonald as he spoke to Donald. 'Constable, tell Mrs MacDonald we'll find her grandson and look into her allegations; however, we are not in a position to do much until the body is found. Thank her kindly for her help.'

Donald dutifully transferred the information, and Father Joseph watched her face toughen, her eyes freeze. She stepped forward and gripped Forbes' lapels, and for a second Father Joseph thought he was going to brush her off. 'The priest may be speaking me true, man, but I think he still speaks me wrong,' she said, staring into his eyes. 'If you have any gift of the sight, you'll know what I'm saying, feel what I'm saying. My grandson was murdered by that hoor he married, and no-one is doing anything about it.' She turned and pointed at Father Joseph. 'And him, that devil, knows of it. I've seen him, in my dreams, dancing lights like fireflies over the hill to carry off my Ewan while every lazy one slept the sleep of drunks and fools. I *saw* you. I *watched* you.' She snapped back to the detective. 'And the whole island knows it too, they know I am not lying. *Do* something, man. Help me.'

She let him go, gathered her shawls about her so fiercely they cracked like sails in the wind, turned her back, and left.

'Poor old soul', said Murdoch, 'she's gone a bit daft.'

Donald bridled at the outsider's insult, but said nothing as they climbed aboard and laughed and waved as the boat crossed the bay and slipped around the lee of the hill. Then he kicked the mooring post and spat into the water.

'What is it, Donald?' asked Father Joseph.

'Just those mainlanders, Father. They think they know it all. People like Mrs MacDonald held this island together through disasters they can't imagine. And they dismiss her as an old fool.'

He stumped off, his big back set against the priest trailing in his wake. They reached the fork in the path that took them separate ways.

'Does that mean you believe her, Donald? About Julia? And about me?'

The constable stopped and turned, a look of horror and confusion on his face. He seemed to gather some thought. 'I'm sorry, Father, I didn't mean to be rude,' he said. 'I think I'm just frightened.'

'It's all right, Donald. That's understandable. Come and see me.'

The man nodded, head hung, and left, striding down the track. Father Joseph watched him, and a thought came to him, a clear bell of insight that had not occurred to him before and made him feel very, very alone.

Mrs MacDonald had indeed had her visions, her antiquated, quaint, superstitious imaginings. And they were true.

V

Ewan's grandmother took to haunting Father Joseph, usually at chapel. She stood at the sheep fank when he arrived, and would be standing there when he left long after the congregation.

Julia she merely tossed a 'Hoor' at when she passed by, bowed, muzzled in her shawl, a lonely figure unsupported. She sat in the front pew, listening dutifully to the priest but never looking up at him. Her family stayed away and, it seemed, no-one else felt the urge to sit beside her, perhaps afraid of the wrath of the old crow outside.

Then Julia simply stopped coming.

Father Joseph went to see her and found her startled and silent. She welcomed him in the most desultory of manners and then sat by the fire. The house remained uncleaned and her meals, if the account of Mairi at the little shop could be believed, would barely feed a sparrow. He visited her, reasoned with her again and again, reminded her of the mortal sin of not attending Mass and left her unconvinced, wasting away because of her husband just as surely as if he'd been there to beat her.

But Mrs MacDonald let her be, and he was thankful for that. His congregation dwindled a little and those who persevered became furtive and shifty: they arrived with their collars turned up and scarves around their faces against the cold, but more against the withering stare of the old woman, as if she wouldn't recognize them beneath their winter clothes. She would tut, occasionally call, 'Still frequenting the House of the Devil, are we, Donald?' or 'Hello Duncan, hello Shona. Do you think worshipping with a murdering priest will bring you luck with your bairns? I doubt it,' and they would shuffle past, quickening their step.

She was untouchable. Immense.

'Mrs MacDonald', he asked her, 'why are you doing this?'

It was raining, cold horizontal slate-grey sheets

that he'd only ever seen on the island. She was soaked through but indomitable, her dark eyes and unsmiling mouth convincing him that she would never, never leave him.

'I want the truth. I know my grandson was murdered. I saw it and I saw you involved in it. I won't rest until it's proved.'

'Please, Mrs MacDonald, try to put this behind you. Ewan is gone and soon we all will leave here. We can feel sad about that, but it must be because of the good we have left behind, not because of any wrongs that have been done. Otherwise, we cannot start afresh.'

'What do I care for the others, for their new life? I gave half my life to this island, cared for them when they were sick, brought their babies into the world. Mine was the first door they called on when the pains began, I was the one who spent night after night tramping these hills to do what was necessary. Not you and your ilk. And for thirty years I have been cast out, rejected. I owe them nothing. I am owed my grandson.'

'I'm sorry. I just think you will make everyone suffer. Is that what you want?'

She stepped closer and peered at him; for the first time he realized he was only an inch or two taller than her. 'No, priest. I don't want everyone to suffer. I don't even want that murdering little hoor my grandson was stupid enough to marry to suffer.' She gave the impression of leaning forward and he instinctively stepped back. 'Just you,' she added. 'I just want you to suffer. And to make sure that happens, Man of God, I promise I will be with you for as long as you live.'

It was age, weakness in him, the stress of the last few months, but his knees buckled and a pain clutched his chest and shot along his arms to his fingertips. He reached out for her shoulder to steady himself; she let him, neither pushing him off nor helping him. The ground swam.

'I ... I'm sorry Mrs MacDonald. I feel unwell. Excuse me.'

Gasping, he pushed himself away from her and stumbled down the hill, feeling her eyes triumphant on his back. He scrabbled his way home, and took to his bed for three days.

The Stewart girl, Morag, fifteen, pretty and simple, came each day to tend him. She was his only visitor. He asked her how the village was, and she said everyone was fine, though Mrs MacDonald was visiting many folk: that new stick of hers certainly helped her get about.

His sleep was fitful and filled with dreams. Julia was brought to him from the Front bleeding and dying as the artillery flashed around them and the whizz bangs crumpled on the turf roof of the trench, and he murdered another young soldier with the face of Ewan, and she revived, and men who wore clean uniforms and who had paunches came to take him away and punish him for it, though he always woke before he found out what his sentence was.

On the second day of his illness he heard a noise through the fog of his fever and, somehow, instantly recognized what was happening. A pail clattered, rusty handle screeching, and the back door opened and shut. He found himself peering out of the window before he was fully conscious. Morag had gone for peat, and he felt sick and giddy with illness and fear and guilt. He watched her short journey up the hillside to the cleit, pail swinging, and watched her come down again, searching her face for signs of discovery. He found none, but saw the suspicion she felt when she returned and found this sick old man, who was the talk of the village and who might have murdered a man, watching her every move.

He was on his feet on the fourth day, though weaker. He went down to the village; no-one stood on the doorsteps, but it was winter, he told himself, despite the feeling that they were closed against him and marks had been placed on the weather-washed doors by some stern prophet to protect the inhabitants from his plague.

He tried to pass the time with Mairi, but she was

busy, sorry Father, she said, and bustled through to the back to take stock of her store-room, a pointless exercise since it would not be replenished before the evacuation in the Spring.

The congregation became more unwilling: they attended Mass faithfully, but their catechisms and hymns were muted, and the confessions were grudging. Why ask forgiveness from a liar, a murderer? For the first time in a long while, he had to admit, he felt the need for confession. Perhaps he had given up his creed long ago, truly. Perhaps he had simply eased into the position, left behind any conviction, any doctrine, for the practicalities of being – a what? – to this community. And now an old woman demanded a truth, a truth that was hers by right, and he couldn't speak to her.

She was unfailing, a pinched black ghost, silently vigilant in her usual place by the wall, so still it seemed she merged into the stanes and the dyke and the tussocks and the hillside, merely one detail in a landscape that stretched into the distance for generations. He was unwell, he could not speak to her, he was simply hallucinating, you're a stupid old fool, he said, unable to stop her getting under his skin.

But he got better, slowly. He managed out of the house more often, walking by the shore, deliberately timing it with the day and the weather so he could catch someone at the boats. He would say hello, ask after their families, and received courteous but cold replies, aye Father, all well for our last winter. He stopped by unannounced at cottages and was reluctantly invited into the warmth of cooking, was told about plans for the evacuation and how children had heard of masters who belted naughty children in the mainland schools, but was never offered dinner. He returned to an empty cottage, his dinner in the stove, left by Morag, and no-one came to call.

This cannot go on, he told himself, cannot go on, but was at a loss as to how it might be ended.

vii

Mrs MacDonald ended it for him. She died.

In the January, he locked the chapel as usual, feeling more dispirited than ever because of the New Year and what it was to bring, and was trudging past the old woman yet again when he heard her cough.

It was a deep racking cough, and he sensed her shudder with the weight of it. He stopped, turned, fought against the optimism he felt welling up inside him and strangled it in order to embrace the concern he should have for her. She looked at him and nodded.

'Aye, priest, you're right. It seems I'm the last one on the island. The last one to have the sight. The last one to suffer the boat cough. The last one to die here.'

'No, Mrs MacDonald, the boat cough's long gone. No-one's had it for nigh on twenty years. It's a touch of the cold you have and, if you'd allow me, I'll take you home. You'll be fine with some care.'

'The Christmas boat came. You know it's from Harris. I've been like this since then. And it was fine when we all got it years ago, for we were younger then, but I won't be able to fight it off at my age. This will be last time I'll be here, Man of God.'

'I'll come to visit you.'

She seemed genuinely surprised. 'I would have thought you would have me damned long ago.'

Father Joseph smiled, though, since Ewan's death, he felt his smiles were always sallow. 'No, Mrs MacDonald, that's far too Presbyterian a way for me.'

She peered at him. 'You're a fool,' she said. 'You know that I could torment you from my bed. I might not stop while you keep my grandson from me.'

'Well, if you'll pardon the expression, we all have our cross to bear. I want to do this.'

She nodded twice, jabbing, bird-like, and he wondered if she took him to be admitting his guilt. Perhaps he was. 'If you must,' she said.

And he walked her home, silent all the road there. As they passed the cottages by the shore, he knew that curtains twitched at their backs and that sighs were being heaved behind those curtains at what would be mistaken for a state of truce.

He attended her every day, spending most of the morning and then returning in the evening. She did not curse but demanded tea with as much bad grace as she could. He offered to read to her, and she snorted with derision, since she had never seen the need for the trick, but he did anyway: not the Bible, but condescending anthropologies of the outer Isles, Harris, and the Monachs, and Rona with its population twice wiped out, and barren little Heiseigger. She never spoke to him during the evenings, only tutted now and again at a particularly stupid notion the Lowland writer had of a local custom or legend, and did nothing to acknowledge him when he left.

Several others came over the fortnight, to pay respects, to see what they could do, but she sent them away angrily: weak and spineless they were. They left with pained faces and returned to chapel, where Father Joseph made them pray for Mrs MacDonald. He sermonized fervently and made them confess mournfully and was sorry for them: they found no peace anywhere, from either the old woman or their demanding priest.

Her last night was wracked with pain: her chest was filled with phlegm but she could no longer cough without sending spasms all the way to her hands and her feet. Her brow was soaked with sweat and spittle gathered at the corners of her mouth, twitching in, out, in, out, with her rasping breath.

'Priest,' she said weakly. 'Come here.'

He folded the towel he was using to dry her supper dish – she had eaten nothing and the soup had gone into the waste bucket – and sat by her bed. 'Yes, Mrs MacDonald?'

She swallowed hard, decisively. 'I want you to do

something for me. Will you do as I ask?'

He felt a dread, a horror that her final request would be to know the truth – I am dying now, I will not live, your secret will die with me, she would say – and he would have to face the awfulness of deciding.

'Yes,' he said, but he was unsure.

'I do not want to be buried on the island.'

He fought down a desire to cry out his relief. 'Mrs MacDonald. You can't mean it. Good grief, woman, you *are* this island.'

'Don't be stupid. You may have believed me capable of such pride, but you are wrong. My grandson is here, unmarked somewhere. I know it. There is no point in denying it, though I will not ask you to confirm it now. I do not want to rest here while he cannot.'

'Oh Mrs MacDonald. This should not be done.'

'Take me to the mainland. I want to be burned. Spread my ashes in the bay. That is what I want.'

A wave of nausea overtook him, and he realized his creed was stronger than he had thought. Why had he been able to conceal a dead man, bury him with the minimum of ceremony, conceal the truth to the point of lying, when the idea of allowing the body of this old woman to be incinerated filled him with disgust?

'I ... I'm sorry. You know I can't do that. Please, ask someone else. Donald, he will help, even though he is Catholic. Or I will arrange it with the authorities. But this is something that is against everything I've ever believed in.'

She said nothing, stared at the ceiling, and he felt as despicable as he could. He had entertained the possibility of redemption for what he had done with Ewan, but he was beyond it for this, for denying this old woman again and again. He tried to coax her, gently, to reconsider. You belong here, he soothed, it is your home, this island needs your spirit, even if it is abandoned. But she would not be moved, would not absolve him.

At two in the morning, she died. She choked and

rasped and he leaned over her.

'Remember now', she whispered, 'as long as you live. I will never leave you.'

viii

Now, Father Joseph and Julia and the ashes of Mrs MacDonald were on the last boat to leave the island. Donald was there too, and the younger members of the community, some of whom had spent the previous night at Sandy's drinking the remaining evidence of a lifetime of criminality in the most pleasurable of manners, though judging by the way many of the men held their heads they were not enjoying it so much now.

The sun slanted low, a fine spring morning with a silver rolling swell, and fast, ethereal clouds. Most, glumly sentimental, looked back at the island for signs of the few sheep and lost cats left behind, or at the roofs, already seeming dilapidated. Some stood at the bows, peering at the horizon, stoical or weary or optimistic. Julia sat amidships. A breath of wind caught him in the eye, spilling water, and he had a kaleidoscopic vision of her, shining bright halos. She looked beatific, poor girl.

His hands were cold on the surface of the urn. It had not been so bad, doing the unthinkable. He had arrived at the decision minutes after the old woman's death, simply and calmly resolving to put aside one more tenet, one more archaic poppycock that he had the audacity to wish to cling to when he had given up so much already. Besides, his flock – the term vexed him – had to leave everything behind: why shouldn't he? And he'd found it relatively easy to put aside his trepidation when he'd arrived on the mainland with the body, in a relatively salubrious hearse, horses' bits chiming in the frosty air, at the tiny red-brick building with the incongruously imposing chimney. The little men in white shirts and blue overalls had doffed their caps, and gingerly, almost tenderly, taken the coffin away. He'd waited outside, gone for lunch at a tea shop on the front and chatted amiably with the bluff, plump, attractive woman who fussed over him and was filled with curiosity about the island: she'd visited it once, she said, on a trip some summers ago.

In the afternoon he'd returned, and the man with the moustache who seemed to be in charge had invited him in for a cup of tea, and his subordinate had brought a bronze urn, surprisingly heavy, and left it discreetly on the occasional table behind Father Joseph's back. When the man with the moustache had politely stood up and reminded him he didn't want to miss the boat, he'd been about to ask where the ashes were, but caught the almost surreptitious gesture which indicated the urn. Remarkable professionalism, he'd thought, for a practice so barbaric. And so compassionate: there will be no charge, Father, the man had said, a favour to yourself and a mark of respect for an old woman without a soul to miss her.

And, for the remaining three months, Mrs MacDonald had been with him, on the crude wooden shelf which served as a mantel, surrounded by as much junk as he could muster so that if something fell and smashed on his floor, it would not be Mrs MacDonald. Visitors had begun to come by again, he was sure, to see the old woman stuffed in her little urn like the pagan genie she might well have been. He'd tolerated their curiosity and made them tea. Julia had stayed away, and he rarely saw her. Each time he did, she and he seemed stronger, a little more placid, and therefore a little more removed. Not that their complicity had ever brought them close, but he felt a vague regret.

The shoreline receded and faces turned away. One by one they caught Father Joseph's eye and gathered, unbeckoned, amidships, some sitting on trunks and chests, some with cardboard suitcases between their feet. They would not allow his final duty to the island to be private. Perhaps rightly so: the old woman was more one of them than he could ever have been. His time on the island had lasted twenty-five years, hers a thousand.

'I do not plan to say any prayers,' he said to them. 'I cannot imagine anyone who would welcome them less than Mrs MacDonald. And I won't make any speeches, other than to say that an island isn't an island without the sea which surrounds it, and Mrs MacDonald chose to be at one with the sea, part of the very thing which defined her island. I think that is fitting for her. So I think it's time to set the old lady free.'

The lid of the jar clinked dully. It was the first time he'd looked inside, and there it was, half a pint of grey dust. Not a hint left of her towering blackness. He raised the jar on an outstretched arm and, behind him, the islanders bowed their heads. 'Mrs MacDonald', he said, to her and to no-one else, 'please believe I never meant you any harm.'

He tipped the jar, shaking a gentle stream of the stuff from its lip. It formed an opaque skin on the water, rolling gently with the swell, trailing out behind the boat as it veered around the lee of the hill into fast currents.

As usual, they hit the south-westerly, and the flag at the top of the mast lurched and died and picked up again, contorting itself in the changing eddies of air. So, too, did Mrs MacDonald. The dregs of the urn tumbled towards the water then wheeled out and away from the boat. Father Joseph watched them, mesmerized at the life they took on, gathering in a skipping windwhirl which whipped upwards and skimmed back towards the boat, an ugly little cloud on his horizon. His jaw dropped, his eyes bulged, and the wind flung Mrs MacDonald back at him, and she smacked him firmly in the face. As he gasped at the audacity of her, he took in – filled his lungs as deep as his soul – a breath of her. He gagged, swallowed hard, washing the dryness and blackness of Mrs MacDonald down, into his belly, where she would nestle and course through his bloodstream and clog his veins and, one day, gleefully stop his heart.

'Oh Julia,' he said, already exhausted by the battle ahead.

The pear

The old woman was dressed in grey. Grey apron and headscarf. Grey knittit stockings that crumpled between the bottom of her grey skirt and the top of her grey boots. Even her skin was grey, furrowed and dusty and parched-field coloured.

Jamie watched her from the corner of the street, peering round the edge of the clinic wall. She dragged the sacks to the front of a ramshackle old table which served as her stall. Four sacks: apples, pears, carrots, potatoes. Whit would the prices be this week? – you could never tell, though it wisnae as bad as abroad. Businessmen were jumping aff the Empire State building in America and, in Europe, ordinary working men like his faither were being paid suitcases of money by the day and it still wisnae enough to buy a bag of sugar. It was better here, the newspapers said.

The old woman didnae see him. He enjoyed that feeling, of seeing but not being seen. He often spied through lightit windows at night, at children straining to dae homework by the gaslight, at faithers asleep in front of the fire, work boots propped against the armchair legs. Most of all, he watched the mothers, bent over sewing or darning, their fingers working steadily, automatically, like machines of levers. Their dresses and blouses fluttered open and closed, open and closed: he felt the curve and heaviness of their breasts, the warm milkiness of their smell, and ached down below. He'd go home and lie awake, feverish and fretful, for hours, rescuing the milky mothers fae Eric Campbell and oncoming trains, and he got worried about how his penis went big and hard.

The old woman filled three small wicker baskets with produce and placed them on the table. She leaned back, her hands on her hips. A lassie, fifteen going on sixteen, pedalled up on a bike, swung onto the kerb and jumped off. Her granddaughter. She helped at the stall every second Friday. Billy Campbell in his class fancied her, but big Gerard Connolly said she was his, he'd had her round the back of the town hall. She was plump and dark haired and Jamie imagined her older.

Across the street, Davie Conroy and two other boys from the year above watched from the cobbler's doorway. Pat appeared behind him, jabbed him in the sides. Jamie pretended to be surprised.

'Gotcha,' he said.

'Aye, so ye did. Eejit.'

'Awright. Whit's goin oan?'

'The vultures ur gatherin.' Jamie nodded over to Davie's group. 'Any minute now.'

'Whit's she goat this week?'

'Aipples, pears, carrots, tatties. Ah fancy a pear.'

Within a few minutes, three other boys had turned up. They would all have to be getting to school soon, so it was time to move. As if on a signal, they thrust out into the street, whistling and sauntering and joking like Jack Buchanans.

'How's it gaun, auld yin?' shouted Pat.

'Aye boays, no bad. Whit can Ah dae fur ye?'

They crowded around the stall, all except one of the older boys who sidled up to the girl and laughed with her and touched her thigh. The boys Oohed and Aahed at the fruit and vegetables, fingering them with their left hands while their rights, pushed to the bottom of their jackets through the unpicked stitching of the pockets, reached out and nabbed what they could.

'Well boays, no a bad spread this week, eh?'

'Cannae afford nuthin though,' said Pat.

Jamie tried to push and jostle his way to the front, but the other boys were bigger by a way. He squeezed through and filched a single pear before it all broke up.

'Sorry, missus. Ma da's goat his books.'

'Aye, mine an aw.'

The old woman commiserated: times were hard.

Still, mebbe their mothers could afford a wee bit later. Aye, mebbe, the boys agreed.

They strolled off around the corner, then hollered and pelted away down Mortimer Street toward the school, ducking round a tram and sticking their tongues out at the passengers. They compared their loot: the old woman was ten apples, twelve pears, three carrots and a potato worse off. No-one could understand Jimmy McGuire's passion for raw root vegetables. Davie reckoned he was a tink and said so.

'Bugger off,' Jimmy said, and heaved up green spit to launch at his feet.

They made it to school with five minutes to spare, though Auld Alexander was already on the steps at the boys' entrance, blackboard pointer rigid behind his back, whistle clamped in his teeth. The boys gathered in the far corner of the playground, over the wall from the girls' toilet block, to hide from him, and the one who distracted the granddaughter was given half an apple and a pear as a reward. Some ate their pickings, juice dribbling down their chins. Jamie shoved his pear into his inside breast pocket, saving it for his supper. Or mebbe he could sell it.

Auld Alexander swung the handbell to call the boys into lines. They stood regimented at the foot of the stairs and peered up at him. After morning prayer – God make us working-class scum subservient wee bastards for another day – Auld Alexander held up his hand for attention.

'Boys, I have an announcement to make. Today, the area is to be graced with the presence of the Duke of Kent, who will be performing some public duties. Perhaps you may have read about his visit in the newspaper.'

No-one spoke. No-one coughed – Auld Alexander hated coughing, said it was a symptom of tuberculosis and therefore of bad breeding.

'Well. Perhaps some of you have never encountered newspapers. Am I right, Conroy?'

Davie jerked up. 'Yessir. That's right sir. Ma da

disnae get wan.'

'Which is why you speak like a guttersnipe, Conroy.' Auld Alexander twitched with disgust. 'The Lord Provost – a personal friend – has told me that the route the Duke will take through the town will bring him past our corner of Mortimer Street. He has asked us to cheer the Duke past, and I have agreed. It is a great honour. We will therefore adjourn to Mortimer Street at nine forty-five, where we will gather on the left side of the street. The staff will supervise you. On the right-hand side of the street, girls from the Mary Street Academy will form their own welcoming committee. I needn't remind you that there will be no fraternization: remember, boys, these are young ladies. We will return at ten fifteen.'

There were several long, slow, quiet intakes of breath. The girls from Mary Street Academy. Girls from posh homes who wore uniforms and had legs and breasts. Girls who pushed their noses in the air when scabby boys like them were around. Girls who came to school in their fathers' motor cars. The boys' own female schoolmates were shadowy wee creatures who only shared class space with them and who never spoke, and if you got close tae them they sometimes smellt of urine. And the boys would have thirty minutes across the street fae the girls fae the Academy: they would be able to poke their tongues out, wink and admire them. It wis a dream come true.

Bryant, their teacher, was young and liberal: he belltit only five or six boys a week. They should have done Maths, but Bryant spent the first hour of the morning talking about the visit. He was a republican, he said. Do not be confused, boys, Royalty is not as important for social cohesion as you are led to believe.

'Kings are not born: they are made by artificial hallucination. So says George Bernard Shaw.'

Jamie chewed his pencil; Bryant looked right at him.

'Of course, Jamie, your father was in the union at the engine sheds, wasn't he? He must have strong views on the monarchy.'

Jamie raised himself. 'No noo, sur. He used tae say the monarchy wur parasites.' He shook his head. 'But no noo.'

'Whyever not, Jamie?' He had that aren't-you-glad-you've-got-something-in-common-with-the-likes-of-me look. Bastard. 'I always thought he was a man of principle.'

'He goat laid aff fur huvin a meetin. Noo ma maw cries him a parasite. He said he wis staunin up fur democracy so she skelpt him.'

Most of the class laughed: Pat behind him gave a friendly punch on the shoulder.

'Ah. Democracy, Jamie. Democracy simply means the people thrashing the people for the people.' He paused to let the importance sink in. 'As Shaw says.'

'Naw he disnae. That's shite.'

There was a single, dangerous second of silence. Course, Auld Alexander would have killed him, grabbed him and stuck him till he bled and died, but Bryant wisnae that type. He wisnae that strong.

'I beg your pardon, Davidson? What did you say?'

'It wisnae Shaw. An' that's no whit he said oanywey. It wis Oscar Wilde. Ma Maw reads aw his stuff tae me. He said democracy's the bludgeoning o the people by the people fur the people.'

'Very clever, Jamie. Very clever.'

Jamie looked up at him. He had a Kelvinside chin and his accent pretended to come from there too. He had that saggy look of someone always greetin and girnin: Christ, Buster Keaton. That's who he reminded Jamie of. And he wisnae feart of someone who hung affa town clocks and shoved custard pies down his long johns.

'Aye sir. Sorry sir.'

'You will be.'

Then, from outside the door, Auld Alexander's handbell called them to order. Jamie kept his head down on the way out, but it didn't matter: he felt the respect around him, that untouchable aura that meant everyone was looking at him and thinking he was great, a Daniel amongst the lions, and he was buoyed up by it. Fuck Bryant. It was worth it.

Auld Alexander stood at the swing exit doors; a pail behind him overflowed with stick things, and Carmichael, spotty monitor, passed one to Auld Alexander each time a boy went by, and the stick thing was handed over. Jamie's turn came soon enough; Auld Alexander held out the stick thing. A flag. A Union Jack, cheap cloth, the colours run into each other, on a bit of bamboo cane.

'Take it, Davidson. Wave it when the Duke passes. You never know, he might look at you.'

Look at you? Whit did that mean? Did it mean the Duke was a miraculous bastard and, in his presence, Jamie Davidson esquire, thirteen, nae joab when he left next year, nae chance wi lassies fae the Mary Street Academy, a faither wi nae joab, would suddenly and miraculously be cured of his shitey existence? If you went doon Mortimer Street a wee way, would ye perchance find yersel in fucking Damascus? Still, Auld Alexander wisnae the type tae treat lightly. 'Thank you, sir,' he said, smiling as insincerely as he could.

They doubled up, two-by-two, and silently filed down the road to Mortimer Street, Jamie aware of some jostling amongst the boys to walk near to him. Auld Alexander and Bryant lined them up neatly, like a school photograph, bigger boys to the back, shelpits like Jamie at the front. Across the street, the Mary Street girls looked over, willowy brown-blazered starlets who examined them as if they were encountering wildlife escaped from the zoo. Davie Conroy managed to thumb his nose at them.

Auld Alexander stood in the road and raised a hand, though the boys knew better than to make a sound. 'Boys. The Duke's procession will be here in approximately seven minutes. On my signal, you will raise your Union Jacks and wave them. I do not wish you to cheer: such displays are vulgar, and I am sure that some of you would take advantage of the anonymity to behave inappropriately. Therefore, I expect silence and eyes front. Is that clear?' There was a general mumbling, like a drone from the distant steel works. 'Good, boys. Now enjoy the occasion: you will remember this day for as long as you live.'

A calm descended on the groups. Every boy stared across the cobbles at the Mary Street girls, and every one of the Mary Street girls looked back with such lack of interest it withered their hearts. Then a roar turned their heads and a BSA motorcycle wobbled into view, followed by two black cars. Jamie was disappointed: he'd half thought he might get his first sight ever of a Bugatti, or even a Hispano Suiza, but English royalty preferred to drive around in Austins. Miserable lot. Auld Alexander flapped about in the middle of the road, ready to give instructions. Jamie looked back at the Mary Street girls.

They were all in left profile, all except one. An older girl, taller then most, at the back. Jamie couldn't really tell what she looked like – they were all in identical uniform, their hair tied up and crammed into brown hats. But her face was different, older, sharper and, as Auld Alexander shouted 'Now boys, wave your flags,' she gently shook her head, staring Jamie straight in the eyes and coaxing him on.

He held the stick down. Auld Alexander scurried onto the pavement to be the first to see the Duke. Around him, bits of cloth fluttered and rustled, the sound of wind in his ears. Jamie's hung around his shin. The girl watched him, smiling and coaxing, smiling and coaxing.

Bryant stood at the opposite side of the group, looking down the road along the front of the boys. 'Davidson!' he called. Jamie swung round. 'Wave your flag, boy. Wave your flag.' Jamie shrugged and scratched an itch on his calf. 'Wave your flag boy. Don't be defiant.'

The girl could tell what was happening. She gave Jamie the slightest nod and he let the cane slip from his fingers. The flag balanced momentarily on its tip, then slowly toppled into the gutter.

Then Bryant flew past Jamie, smirking like a bastard, and tapped Auld Alexander on the arm. Snitch. Auld Alexander seemed confused momentarily, looked down the street to see how near the procession was, then pushed past Bryant, gown flapping.

'Davidson. What's the meaning of this? Wave your flag, boy, the Duke is almost here.'

Jamie felt his jaw push out slightly, like he had nae control over it, and he scuffed his feet. Auld Alexander practically jumpt up and doon.

'Davidson! The Duke! The Duke, boy!'

'Fuck the Duke. Fuck yersel an aw.'

It lookt as if Auld Alexander's face was gonnae explode. The other boys stopped waving. 'Keep those flags going, boys! Or there'll be hell to pay!'

Nervously, they began again. And in amongst all the flapping and dancing pennants, Jamie saw the pointer raised. Auld Alexander brought it down across Jamie's chest: he doubled over, and was caught by the nape of the neck and swung around. The pointer smacked him hard across the buttocks, again, again, again, again. Jeesus, it wis sore, it was fucking agony, he felt his insides swell up and the world was pushing out of his arsehole, the wood thwacking hard against bone, Auld Alexander screaming, 'Davidson! Davidson!' at the top of his voice.

And yet there wis a dim pleasure, a sensation of bringing to life those down-below bits he was told to never touch, that and the knowledge of whit it must look like tae the fucking Duke, this wee band of merry boys waving thur flags and in the middle this demented auld bastard battering the living daylights out of one of the loyal subjects of the realm. Clap that chappie in the Tower! Christ, it wis almost funny.

The procession passed: the other boys still waved their flags, terrified tae stop. Bryant the Republican hero hud fucking legged it. Auld Alexander hudnae seen the Duke after all. He whirled Jamie round: there wis sweat on his top lip and he wis breathing heavily. The pointer wis still raised: he looked like a fisherman about tae cast.

'Davidson. Davidson,' he whispered. Then he moved aside, mair stooped and aulder than ever.

The girls from Mary Street had averted their eyes, heads together, twittering and gossiping. The girl in the back row leaned out over them, craning her neck like a swan over those in front of her, looking down the street at the disappearing rear of the Duke's Austin. She had missed it. Or ignored it. Or chose to let him think that.

There was no kudos on the way back to school, no sign that he had taken on the system and won. If anything, his classmates edged away from him, as if he had some disease. The disease of being caught. He walked reasonably well, though his backside felt as if it had been tattooed with strips of hot candlewax and he had to splay his legs out a bit to ease the pressure of his trouser legs on his skin.

Along Mortimer Street, the trees dappled light onto the cobbles, making each one seem perfect in its roundness, its texture. Jamie breathed in. Usually, some factory could be tasted on the air, but he only smellt cleanness and aliveness. Fuck, he ached and ached but he'd been turned on, like a wireless set, glowing and receptive and red, red hot. He loved it.

The classroom was subdued. 'Get your Mathematics books out,' said Bryant. He avoided Jamie's gaze, in fact he avoided looking at the whole class, jist goat his nose stuck in the book and startit reciting questions and answers that they wur supposed tae follow. Jamie snaked his jacket off and shoved it under his bum as a cushion on the hard wooden bench. The pain eased slightly, but a lump in the pocket bumped against his knee.

He fished in: the pear. He examined it under the desk. One single gash, from Auld Alexander's first swipe across his chest, cut the skin. The white flesh oozed. He ran his fingers over the curves of the pear, its smoothness, the rough little bump of the base, the little wrinkled nipple at the stalk. The flesh was flecked with creamy freckles, tiny, tiny flakes suspended in the fruit. Already, the edges of the slash were turning mushy brown.

He slid the pear into his desk. Let it rot. Its weal would moulder, decay, the whole thing would stink and split. His wounds would heal. And he didn't give a shit about the girls from the Mary Street Academy. Or Bryant. Or Auld Alexander.

Oscar Wilde? Fuck aye.

Neighbourly

He was at it again. Vera could hear the pick-pick-pick over the back garden hedge, metal against stone, on and on. It drove her mad. The Andersons who'd lived there before hadn't been like this. They'd been nice neighbours: Susan, their toddler, used to come over to talk to her 'Auntie Weera', the wee soul. She must have left school by now.

'He's at it again,' she called through.

'What?'

'The man over the garden hedge. Jeffries. He's at it again.'

'At what again?'

'Digging. Lots of digging.'

'Who are you talking about?'

'Oh for God's sake, Tom.'

She snatched up the kettle, drove it under the thundering cold-water tap and filled it, splashing everywhere. Men. Bloody stupid men. No better than babies.

She took the tea through to him. He sat, portly, gnomic, peering up at her through his dark-lensed, bottle-top glasses; of course she felt sorry for him, his eyesight so poor now, but he did play on it sometimes. 'Here,' she said, thrusting the cup at him. 'Do you want some tea?'

He opened his mouth. He didn't have his bottom set in, and a thin, glistening thread of dribble connected his top lip to the line of his lower gum. 'Aye. Thanks.' He took the cup, his hands trembling, swung it away from him to the arm-table at his left, swept away the pile of used tissues he collected at his side and rattled the cup down onto the formica surface. 'Thanks. Thanks.'

She often wondered where he'd gone to. He certainly wasn't here any more. Old fool. She blamed herself often for it. No foresight. Her mother had told her: men either bugger off and leave you or they turn into old fools. Toothless. Like children. And you can't get out of it then. Her mother had, got out of it early, chucked her father as soon as she found out he was chasing after that bit of skirt down the pub, and then they'd lived in one rented room after another, never longer than six weeks at a time until she was fifteen and said she wanted to live with her grandmother. Suit yourself, her mother had said. You'll be sorry.

'Who were you talking about, Vera?'

She huffed and grunted. She felt her jaws clamp with rage at having to explain once more, knowing she would have to go through it all again in a couple of hours. 'Jeffries. The man across the back hedge. He's digging.'

'What's he digging?'

'I don't know. I keep telling you. I don't know. He's been at it for three days now and I keep telling you. If he's building a garage, he hasn't got our permission and the drainage will be ruined and it'll flood our back garden.'

He leaned forward, summoning up a glimmer of the strength of will she'd first found attractive, though in their middle years it had made her feel uneasy. 'Why didn't you tell me about it?'

'Oh, Tom, I did. I've been telling you for days.'

'You'd better do something about that.'

'Why me? Why not you? It's always left to me .'

'I can't go.'

'Why not? I'm getting on too, Tom. I can't do everything.'

He gripped his left wrist in his right hand, began to shake. 'I can't. I can't go out the house any more.'

'You can. The doctor says it's all in your mind. You're old, Tom, you're not dead. You sit there all day and brood about yourself. All you ever think about is yourself and I have to do everything. You should start thinking about other people instead of getting wrapped up in yourself.'

'No', he said, 'leave me alone.' The trembling was worse. In a minute he'd start hyperventilating and she'd have to spray under his tongue or she'd be at the hospital all night again and they'd let him out in the morning and say

'Panic attack.'

'You do, Tom. There are children worse off than you, but you sit and brood.'

He shambled onto his feet. 'I'm going upstairs. I'm going to lie down.'

'Oh for God's sake, Tom!'

She wouldn't see him for an hour or so, and then she'd hear the dull thump of the shoe on the floor. She would go up to him and he'd be hanging half in, half out of the bed, and he would ask for help to get up, in that pathetic, wee boy voice, even though they both knew he could manage himself if he really tried.

Her son didn't understand. He came round, very occasionally, and she would try to tell him, try to tell him just how much she had to bear, how his father couldn't remember what day it was, how he accused her of leaving him, how he imagined men coming into the house in the evening when he was in bed and interrogated her for hours afterwards. Her son would sigh, say he's old and refuse to speak while he did some little odd job around the house.

Why wouldn't he listen?

Yet he would sit and talk to the old man, listen to his ravings about the War, working in the quarries, long-dead workmates. He would nod his head and look interested, even though she knew he'd heard it, for God's sake, dozens and dozens of times before. And when she corrected some stupid notion – 'No, Tom', she'd say, as patient as she could, 'that wasn't in 1958, we weren't even living there in 1958' – her son would sigh and mutter something about it not being the point and look away out of the window. 'And what is the point?' she'd ask him, and he'd say, 'It doesn't matter, Mum.'

Were men in it together?

She took up her knitting, a little jacket for Sally across the road, nice girl, expecting her first in six weeks. Sally was a nurse, came over and looked after Tom when he was found on the living room floor, almost dead, after his third heart attack. Gave him the kiss of life. She'd shuddered as she watched the girl, blonde hair falling over the old man's face, wondering how could she? Not the sort of thing she'd have done. At that age.

The needles clicked furiously, dipping, spearing. The cat prowled in and sat at her feet, watching the movement. 'Don't you dare,' she threatened. She'd had the cat fourteen years now, ever since Theresa from up the road had thrust a tiny tabby into her arms after her ginger tom was run over. Morgan, it'd been called. It had dragged itself back to the house, smashed to pulp, back legs gone, the side of its face all bloody and split, looking for all the world like a pomegranate. It'd messed itself as well: the smell was putrid. They'd heard it howling on the doorstep, a mad whine, then found it bleeding all over the brown hairy doormat with 'WELCOME' on it, and she held her son back while Tom pushed it off the doorstep with his foot into the herbaceous border under the front room window and took a brick to its head. He didn't even discuss getting the vet.

The tabby meowed. 'What is it darling?' she asked. It blinked its heavy lids lazily at her. Hungry. 'Okay then. Let's get you fed.'

She led the way, the tabby, fat and diabetic, weaving a tenuous path behind her. In the kitchen she opened a tin of an expensive fish recipe – all the wee thing could keep down, she told Mrs MacKenzie in the shop – and filled the blue plastic bowl. The cat sniffed once and turned away. 'Always stick your nose up, don't you?' she said. It looked over its shoulder at her. It would come back. Later.

And there it was again, the regular clank of that bloody man, digging. Digging what, for Christ's sake?

She yanked the back door open and looked down her garden. The hedge at the bottom was neatly trimmed on her side but, half way across its depth, it sprouted up untidily. She'd tried to tell him, once when she met him in the supermarket, about his responsibilities towards its upkeep, had even offered to give him the telephone number of her gardener who could come round with his long ladders and trimmer and cut the top. He'd looked at her as if she was stupid, though if anyone lacked a bit of basic common sense and intelligence it was him. An insurance salesman, that's all he'd been. Pensioned off. On the sick.

The wall of privet was too thick to see through, though she had an impression of a mound growing higher on the other side. She wouldn't allow it. Those pigs who used to live next door, the Abercrombies, had put up a shed on a concrete base and the autumn rains had come and washed away everything from her garden, the pansies and forsythia and clematis, piled up against the windbreak that hid the side of the house from prying eyes. There'd been a clay-coloured stain six feet wide across her lawn. She'd stopped that nonsense, got it moved, the base broken up. She wasn't going to let anything like that happen again.

The cat ambled out between her legs before she slammed the door shut. A hook on the inside held her jacket, an old green anorak she kept for the gardening. It would do. She locked the back door, went through the house to the entrance hall cupboard, put on her shoes, listened for a second to check on Tom, then left by the front door.

Jeffries' house was easy enough to find: she got her bearings, walked round the block into the almost identical street at the back of her own and counted along. His, though, was shabbier than her own. The curtains and windows needed a good wash, she reckoned, and the window sills peeled four or five coats of paint. There was no answer when she rang the doorbell, so she squeezed past the old foreign car in the driveway and headed around the back. Weeds poked through the grey stone chips.

The back garden was a shambles: at the bottom, next to the hedge bordering her own house, were two parallel mounds of earth, four feet high, fifteen feet long. Soil spilled over the lawn and paths mingling with the bags and piles of clothes and odd articles – a mirror, a record player – strewn all over the place.

It occurred to her a split second after she called 'Hello' as loudly as she could that he might have murdered someone and was in the middle of burying the body: what she knew of his history grabbed her by the throat and she almost fainted. His wife had left him years ago – or had she? And no-one had seen his daughter for a while – her hand flew to her mouth – and it was all so strange. She would leave, she decided, get her lawyers onto this.

She turned and collided with him as he came out of the porch from the house. He started, seeming very put out. She looked at his shabby grey trousers and dirty white vest and resisted the urge to brush herself down.

'Can I help you?' he said, squinting. 'Was it you at the front door?'

There would be no point pretending she had come round for a cup of sugar. She took a step back and squared her shoulders.

'My husband,' she began, and found her throat was dry and her words sounded squeaky, not at all the sort of voice to take command of a face-to-face situation with a man who might be a murderer. She coughed. 'My husband and I are concerned about your digging. We don't want it interfering with our drainage. I said to him I'd come round and check out what you were building.'

He looked at her with the same vacant expression he'd had that time at the supermarket. Then he shrugged. 'I've not done anything wrong.'

She wasn't reassured, but thought it would be a good idea to suggest that she was. 'I never said you had. I never thought for a minute ... it's just, as I said, we ...'

'I'm not building anything.' He brushed past her. Whatever he was up to – and she could tell it wasn't right – he didn't seem all that bothered about her knowing. He walked to one end of the hole, then turned and stepped down a slope between the mounds, disappearing from view bit by bit, his head at last bobbing down behind the bank of soil.

She was in two minds. Sense, of course, dictated

that she should go now, and report the nasty little man to the police. On the other hand, even though he was fifteen years younger than her, he was podgy and unfit. Given that he was down the hole, if she should creep up and look in, he'd never have time to catch her if she saw something she shouldn't and had to make a run for it.

She tiptoed to the edge and looked over, almost falling in with shock. He had excavated a hole at least six feet deep and more than three times as long, inclining it towards the deep end like a swimming pool. A wheelbarrow leaned over on its side half way down the slope. At the bottom, the little man shovelled dirt on top of a half-buried pile of furniture – an orange mattress underneath a cheap, white-laminate chest of drawers that looked ready to topple.

The man was obviously insane; she tried not to ask, but she couldn't help it. 'Just what, exactly, are you doing?'

He blinked upward into the sunlight at her back, mole-like. He stopped scraping. 'It's none of your business. This is my garden. Go away.'

She felt her mouth pursing. 'I've been trying to tell you. It *is* my business. What you do here can affect my garden. Now, what are you doing?'

'I don't want to discuss it. It's private.'

'Do you want to discuss it with the police?'

He lifted his head again. His eyes were pale and watery and she was completely taken aback when a huge tear flopped out and down his cheek.

'Go ahead. Call them if you want. I did.' He plonked down onto the mattress, his pot belly turning him into a miserable and pathetic little Buddha. 'It's my daughter. Judith,' he said. 'She's gone. Police won't look for her.'

'Why not?'

'She's sixteen. Over the age of consent. Say they can't force her to keep in touch with me if she doesn't want to.'

'Where is she?'

'With her mother. Twelve years I've looked after

her, since ... her mother walked out. And she comes back out of the blue and tells Judith some lies and shows pictures of big hotels in London and ...'

He stopped, choked on the words. He pulled a handkerchief out of his pocket and wiped under his glasses, smearing the dirt on his face into muddy streaks. 'I asked her not to go. But she says she's bored, just like her mother was, and she's not coming back. Don't worry, I says, you won't get back in here if you walk out that door, so she says there's no point writing then, and that was three months ago now.'

'Do you know where they went?'

He shook his head. 'London, maybe. But could be anywhere. They might've moved on.'

For a long while, she didn't know what to say. The man seemed as if he was on the point of collapsing inside, just giving up and crumpling before her eyes. And if that happened, what would she do then?

'Well', she said, 'I'm very sorry. I hope you hear from her soon.'

He drew himself up. 'It's her decision. I'm not going chasing after her. Little madam.'

'Yes,' she said. 'Children. They're all the same nowadays.' There was a silence which she found awkward, and she realized she was being invited to leave. 'Well then, I'd best be going. I hope you don't mind, but we were worried. About our garden I mean. Maybe you could make sure it doesn't ... you know ... interfere.'

'Don't worry,' he said, without looking at her. 'There'll only be a bit of soil left over. I'll level it off and spread the extra around the borders.'

'Right. Right. Thank you.'

She stepped away and the man disappeared from sight. She looked around at the bags of clothing, a canvas sack full of teddy bears – a pink rabbit waggled its ears at her – and bits and pieces of posters and magazines. She scuffed a pile of paper and realized it was a bundle of photographs.

She bent down and picked one out. A girl's face,

fourteen or so, beamed at her, healthy and pretty and mischievous, her school tie slightly askance. It reminded her of someone. The girl's look suggested nothing more than perkiness, her mouth wide in a smile and her eyes blue and kindly. I'm happy, it said.

The girl was just a little younger than she'd been when Tom, demobbed and handsome in his navy uniform, had noticed her serving in the teashop in Argyle Street, and set about wooing her with nights at the pictures and the occasional pair of stockings.

Without knowing why, she unzipped her jacket and slid the photograph inside. Silly really.

She was back home inside ten minutes, let herself in the front door, hung her jacket in the hall cupboard, put on her slippers and went straight upstairs to her small boxroom at the back of the house. She pushed the photograph into her bedside cabinet drawer, amongst the old birthday cards and letters she was determined she'd clear out some day. Old junk.

Tom was up again: when she went down to the living room, he was sitting in his usual place, bent forward, his hand shoved up under his vest and massaging his heart. To keep the pacemaker going, he said, the battery's almost packed in. She knew that was rubbish: the doctor had told him several times before, they don't run down. Ever.

She crossed the room, aware of his eyes on her. She sat in her chair, picked up her knitting. 'Do you want some tea?' she asked.

He leaned forward. 'Where have you been? I had to get up all by myself.'

'I went round to see that Jeffries man.'

'Who?'

'Mr Jeffries. The neighbour over the back.'

'I don't know him.'

'Yes you do. The one who's digging.'

'Digging? No, I don't know anyone who's digging.'

'Oh, Tom. We spoke about him earlier. About our

garden getting flooded. You told me to do something about it, so I went to see him.'

'I never did.'

'Tom, you did . You sat there and told me to do something about it.'

His hand was gripping his wrist now. 'I did not. Why are you telling lies about me?' The shuddering began, gently. 'Who is this man? The Andersons, they live in that house. There's no man there.'

Her teeth clenched and she sighed loud and angrily. She lowered her head and click-clicked her needles, just failing to drown out the sound of his gasping breath.

business

i never meant what happened
i just stopped because of the lustre jug in the front room window blue and white patterned it was i saw it through the curtains and thought it might be worth something and business has been slow in the shop an antique shop used to be my fathers but he died last year and what with the recession no ones buying anything any more i have to keep my eye out for good bargains i try not to be like the sleaze merchants who spend all day long targeting the sheltered housing you know using a penny stall figurine to get in the door and then pay a tenth to clear out all the best items like that bastard davidson he once got an old covenantors chest complete with documented history for forty quid when it was worth at least five hundred or maybe six its not my fault its just dead easy to get through the front door all you do is appear interested in the story not the jug like i couldnt help noticing you have one my mother had one too you know but i broke it packing when she died could you tell me where you got it i only thought you could get them in england oh you are english how interesting
and thats you in
see cause old people love telling their stories it doesnt matter what they part with if you give them a chance to relive a bit of their lives theyll sell their grannys heirloom for a song and frequently do in fact one old woman gave me her grannys heirloom so that she could sing and id listen some old song about somebody called barbara and unrequited love and red roses and briars and i said how sweet it was as i went out the door with two hundred quids worth of silver teapot under my arm just for listening intently and eating a fig roll with a cup of earl grey
so anyway there i am and i should give it my all because the old guys got some really nice stuff especially some meissen and a writing desk that must be early nineteenth century or

older if i can get a good look but yes he says his father bought the jug eighty three years ago and even then it was expensive oh four guineas perhaps and im nodding but disconnected somehow like im not really there which isnt like me when im on the scent and then that dog of his stupid poodle starts yapping squealing more at me as if im paying any attention to it i couldnt give a shit and it scuttles under the table which ive got my eye on too because its a really spectacular mahogany and the old guys quite upset trixies never like this he says and shes such good company since his wife died and when he talks his false teeth rattle around and he gets down on his knees clicking his tongue and leaning under the table to encourage the dog out

well i dont know why

i just suddenly felt so tired i didnt feel violent or any hatred christ i didnt even know him but just the heat getting to me and the dust smelling musty like old folk and looking down at him on all fours like a dog and hearing that poodle just yapping away i reached down and grabbed his belt at the back of his trousers and he was surprised and went to say something and i caught hold of his collar greasy with brylcreem and yanked his head up of course he was half way under the table and the back of his head

cracked
against the underside
and there was this thud
and a splintering sound
and he groaned and went heavy

i let him go and he sort of crumpled and i looked at him and he seemed like a bagful of washing for the laundry i couldnt do anything i mean he was dead there wasnt any point crying over spilt milk so i took a look around and he really had some nice stuff even a couple of watercolours worth a few hundred and a writing case he kept under his bed for some reason that had some brilliant inlay there were some old dresses in the wardrobe probably his wifes particularly this black satin one with thin shoulder straps and sequins and a skirt that flared out any female would look a doll in i even had a look through his kitchen press and right at the back on the floor under the shelves he had this chest of old tools he must have been a carpenter because they were that kind of gear planes and wood chisels and things and they were all pristine like hed not wanted to get rid of them and spent years polishing them up and treasuring them yeah his own personal treasure chest thats what it felt like and for a while it was dead quiet like the only sound was this grandfather clock ticking and a game show going on in a flat upstairs but then i heard this slurping and then a weird noise like someone hauling themselves upstairs when its really an effort for them and i went back to the front room and the old bastard was still alive must have been really tough a real mans old man as my mother would have said and he was sitting there holding his head in his hands and there was this wound over his ear like a flap of skin had been peeled back and underneath was white like milk there wasnt much blood just a few like big pinpricks which looked even more disgusting i reckoned and his wee dog was licking his chin standing up on its back legs its front paws on his chest and it must have woken him brought him round licking his face and he looked at me stupid like hed just woken up after sleeping really late his eyes were staring and blank and his mouth was open and i noticed his teeth were out lying under the table they must have fallen when he hit his head

i couldnt let this go on i mean he was really suffering

and everything was going so well

i remembered a hammer in the tool chest really nice one with a lovely dark wood handle and a heavy claw so i went and got it and came back and the old guy still just looked at me holding his head and he trusted me i mean he looked at me as if i could help him even though he didnt know what the matter was even when i lifted the hammer and i couldnt do it him sitting there like a kid with his wee dog in his lap and i had this feeling of panic for a second like what the fuck was i going to do now but somebody up there must like me because he sighed let out this one long deep breath that came from god knows where and he lay down keeled over but gentle like lay his head against the wooden foot of the table leg and just died i was sure this time because nobody breathes out like that and the pinpricks of blood began to gather and seep into his hair and this tiny pool appeared underneath his head staining the carpet his wee dog whimpered and i kicked it in the rib cage really hard so that it wouldnt interfere it went bowling into the corner of the room and i brought my heel down on its head

just once though

and it shut up then

anyway i went about my business what id come here for although things had turned out a bit different from what id planned and i got a couple of pillowcases for the small stuff like the writing case and a couple of bits of meissen i wrapped them in old shirts i took the dress although i couldnt sell that anywhere but i liked it id imagine someone in it someone id really want to be with because its pretty i found his keys i didn't know if id be able to come back later for the bigger stuff but it was worth thinking about all depended on how quickly i could move once id left but i did feel that this was all mine not a power kick like but just that id inherited it that someone was going to have it so why not me then i thought about taking the tools theres actually quite a market for old craft stuff and i took a look in the chest then remembered the hammer and went back to the living room because id put it on the table while i was seeing to the dog and i suddenly wondered about the hammer and the handle and fingerprints so i wiped it carefully on the tablecloth really did it thoroughly but i was worried so i took it to the kitchen sink and washed it then of course i started worrying about the washing up liquid bottle

so i wiped that and all round the sink where else did i touch i thought dead stupid of me but i couldnt be sure

the wardrobe door

the table edge
the shelvcs in the press
i even wiped the leather belt around the old guys trousers took me ages to fix it all but in the end i felt satisfied id got the lot

and then the other worries started really crazy things like how much can they tell and i went down on my knees at the doormat to make sure the imprint of my shoe wasnt there and i inspected the dogs head just in case there was a tread mark that would give me away my head started aching with it all but i had to be sure and i got the vacuum cleaner out and hoovered the place walking backwards all the time to pick up after me as i went all the way to the kitchen press where it was kept and i was going to take my shoes off but then i thought about the fibres in my socks getting into the carpet then i had an idea i took them off and slipped a couple of plastic carrier bags over my feet because i could walk about the place safely and then take them with me after id done that i should have felt safe because id decided i wasnt coming back and jesus i realised i couldnt take anything absolutely fuck all and i just dumped the pillowcases on the bed and did a final check to get the fuck out but things kept swirling about in my head i couldnt stop them and it was getting so late because i could hear the ice cream van jingling down the street and the sun was dead low orange like coming in through the front room window showing up the dust drifting around the room and i remembered someone saying once that dust was just dead skin from people and how far have they got with that dna business and how much of this was me and i just sank on to my knees to think what i could do about this and it

just
wasnt

fucking

fair

How will you grieve?

The hospital lobby's empty. The WRVS shop's closed. The cafeteria's deserted; I took my father in there last week, down six floors in the lift. We sat at a table by the window and had watery hot chocolate and I bought him a packet of soft chewing mints, helped him back to his room, said cheerio. He thought he'd been to the shopping centre on the other side of town. Then he got too sick to get out of bed.

Somewhere in the building a floor polisher hums and chanks softly. A blue-dressed nurse hurries across the hall, far in front of me. She half turns. She's been crying, her eyes are red and puffy. 'Isn't it so sad?' she says, and disappears down a corridor signposted 'radiology'. I nod. I suppose it is, though I didn't know what to feel when the doctor asked me to sign the form. I get to the exit doors without seeing anybody else. They swish open.

I've been up all night and I'm knackered. I wait for a bus, leaning against the pole, my knees feeling like water, but after twenty minutes there's no sign of one. I set off down the hill, turn right, head through the traffic lights at Maxwellton and on up into the West End and the High Street, down New Street. It's grey today. The rain's misty and horizontal. It seeps through my jacket. I'm soaked inside a quarter of a mile.

No-one's about. Now and again a taxi passes, in the wrong direction for me. Anyway, I haven't got enough for the fare. No cars. No pedestrians. Weird. The windows of flats are open, though. Some choral music overflows from some, pouring down the walls of the buildings, settling on the blue-green-shiny puddles in the gutter.

I'd spoken to my father only yesterday morning. He asked me who I was. After I told him, he whispered, 'I've had enough. My mind plays such tricks on me, you wouldn't believe it, wouldn't believe it.'

'Och don't be daft, dad,' I told him. 'You'll live to be

a hundred.'

'Wouldn't that be something,' he said. 'I'll get a telegram from the Queen.'

'More like King Charles by that time,' I reckoned.

In his town, he said, in Poland, 1923, there'd only been two other Evalts, like him. One reached a hundred. He'd been so proud just to share the old man's first name. There'd been celebrations for a week, parties and civic receptions. People invited the old man to tea, hoping his good luck would rub off on their homes. Young couples went to his house, asked him for his blessing, and he waved his hand over them and kissed them both on the cheek. My father'd gone with his girlfriend, and Evalt the Elder had smiled and his beard was dappled with crumbs of food and smelled of chewing tobacco. My dad and his girlfriend split up a year later, just before Evalt the Elder died in his sleep.

The other Evalt was a trapeze artiste. His circus travelled for most of the year, came back in the spring. First up was a huge pole, twenty feet tall, topped with a platform no bigger than a gramophone record cover, and Evalt the Acrobat would shimmy up on a rope and spend all day performing handstands and backflips, his red and blue and yellow costume flashing like a humming bird while the rest of the troupe helped erect the marquee. When evening came and the crowds arrived for the first performance of the season, Evalt the Acrobat came down from his perch and strode towards the tent without a word, and climbed straight up to his swing and made the audience gasp with his leaps and twirls. Later, he came into town with the crew and the strongman and they drank themselves into oblivion and found some men to fight.

'He was like aristocracy,' my father said. Then he asked me where I worked, how I made my living. 'I work in the bank, Dad,' I said. Been there for nine years, but I didn't remind him of that.

Pubs are locked, jeweller's shops are unlit, dogs sniff at black bin bags of rubbish abandoned on the pavement. A neutron bomb's gone off. I cut through the new shopping centre, dark, deserted. My father loved to shop, changing labels on suitcases so he got leather ones for the price of vinyl. He took me up to Glasgow when he came home from building oil rigs and nuclear power stations, to the old John Lewis. He'd start off in the jewellery section on the upper floor, fingering the watches. I was desperate for one of the flashy Timexes, but he never had the money, and the twenty-one-jewel automatics he stole, flicking them expertly into his inside jacket pocket while the attendant was busy, were sold to his workmates at Nigg or Hunterston. Then I followed him down the wooden-slatted escalator and round the delicatessen, watching his gnarled, twisted old hands, his knuckles swollen from the wartime frostbite he got on the Russian Front, and he'd buy Hungarian salami and Polish bread and jars of rancid Sauerkraut. I was terrified he'd get caught, those big round black cameras like Dalek heads in the ceiling following him around, but he did it right. If he'd left straight away, made a bolt for the door, someone would have stopped him.

Fly man, my dad.

There are escalators in here too, gleaming steel, yellow danger lines. They're not moving. I clump up them, the step a bit too unfamiliar for a comfortable stride. At the top, in the wall of the entrance hall, there's a plaque. Flowers are strewn around it, bunches and bunches, carnations and gypsophila and all sorts. It's awash with them.

I remember my dad met a princess here once. There were crowds of folk, but he got to the front, shouted her over. He shook her gloved hand and said 'Nice to meet you,' and she thanked him for coming to see her, and a guy in a suit touched her elbow and she moved on. 'What was she like?' I asked him, even though I'd already said she was a blonde bimbo and I didn't agree with royalty anyway. Parasites.

'Gorgeous,' was all he said.

People have left flowers where my dad met a princess.

There's movement behind me. A girl and a man. They've black arm bands and plasticked identity badges. The girl's beautiful, blonde-haired, strong-jawed, full lips. She's wearing cream-coloured jeans and a bomber jacket. The guy's more rumpled, a waistcoat like a fisherman, green with lots of pockets. He carries a huge camera, dangling from his right hand like one of my dad's dodgy suitcases.

'Excuse me,' she says, a Stornoway voice that reaches inside and just melts me. 'I'm Elaine Hunter. I'm from BBC Scotland. Could you spare a word?'

I open my mouth, but my throat's dry, like plaster. I make a croaking sound that she thinks is yes. She nods to the guy with the camera. He hoists it up onto his shoulder and a red light comes on. Sniper's nightsight.

Elaine smiles at me sadly and kindly: it feels as if she's interested. I look at the microphone, feel myself falling into it, swirling over and over, black, glossy, textured like the eye of a fly.

'Now sir', she says, hushed, 'how will you be remembering her today?'

I don't understand what she's saying: 'What?' I ask her, then remember my manners, be polite Dad used to say, and 'Pardon?' comes out of his mouth, not mine.

'How will you grieve?'

My head lowers, turns right and left, looks behind. I'm standing in the middle of the flowers. They dazzle me. A chrysanthemum's strayed, petals under my shoe. Pale pink juice oozes from beneath my sole.

I look into the camera, see myself fish-eyed in the lens. My jaw drops, my whole face collapses. There is something sharp and hot in my eyes. Fuck: it spills out and scalds my cheeks. I gulp in a breath and it catches, vocalizes itself into something like a quiet wail. I can't stand this, and I just want to sleep and I slip down onto my knees amongst all the flowers and sob. The scent changes, transforms itself, and I'm burying my face in his jackets, shirts, all I can smell is that old man smell, aftershave and wardrobe and skin.

Elaine says 'Oh dear,' and puts a hand on my shoulder. 'Don't worry, we'll all be okay.'

I catch her wrist in my hand, press my cheek against her knuckles. She uses hand cream. I'm worried about my stubble scratching her perfect skin. She squeezes once, then draws her hand away, turns to the cameraman. He gives her a thumbs up and they stride off, excited, chattering: '... great shot ...' I hear him say, and she says something about a break on national news.

I watch their backs. Elaine's hair picks up her rhythm, switching heavily from side to side. She's content, happy: I can tell. She moves like a cat.

I'm all snottery, stupid, and through the tears the Radio Rentals shop's multiplied, over and over and over. Their TVs are on. A crowd stands silently in front of some iron gates. Flowers everywhere. The sound's turned down, but I bet it's sad.

Someone else must have died.

Finders keepers

Reeds bristled through an edging of ice and the river's centre was sluggish and black. Along the far bank, the slaughterhouse stank and a small steam engine clanked and billowed its way into one of the steel works This side of the river, marshy for most of the year, was undeveloped apart from the little timber merchant's yard a few hundred yards back where Robert found the kitten, ginger and bedraggled and spitting. He clutched it to his chest as it mewed and squirmed inside his coat: he reached in a mitt and tickled it.

There was nothing to do. He got tired of kicking his way through the powdery, frosted grass and perched on the stump of an old iron-topped mooring post, drumming his heels against the dark, slimy wood. He pulled out the kitten and set it on the ground. It teetered a little, found its feet and pounced on something invisible, its tiny caterpillar tail wagging fiercely. Robert wondered how he was going to smuggle it past his mother, since she would know he hadn't been at school as soon as she saw it. His brow furrowed and his lips pursed, his whole face contorting into the scowl his mother said would stay on his face if the wind changed. She was stupid.

Of course, his father would be told if she found out. She would wait until he had sledged his way through his stew and potatoes, mumbling and complaining about the short time at the foundry, and when he was satisfied and belching loudly by the fire she would slyly inform him that his son had been playing truant from school again and how it was disgraceful that a boy of eight could be so wilful and disobedient. His father would feel obliged to remove his belt, and Robert would silently bend himself over the chair and wait for the blows.

From the direction of town, two figures approached along the towpath. Robert recognized them, even from a distance: the Coyles, fourteen and sixteen, big boys who lived across the street. Unlike most of the children of his age, Robert wasn't afraid of them. They weren't really malicious and bullied out of boredom. Their parents were loud and loose-mouthed and hosted parties that went on into the dead of the night: Robert spent hours watching them from his bedroom window, catching glimpses of dancing feet and bare arms and raised glasses. Still, the boys had to be treated warily, so he bundled the kitten up, stuffed it inside his coat and hoped they weren't bored today.

'Hey, Bobby, whit ye daein?' called Brendan, the younger and slower of the two.

'Nuthin.'

'Nuthin? Neither ur we: dae ye want tae come wi us?' Robert shook his head: if he feigned a huff, they might move on. 'Ur ye awright?'

'Aye, fine.'

'No very talkative,' said James. 'Want a nut?'

He took two large walnuts from his pocket, placed them edge on edge in his big apprentice foundry worker's hands and cracked them expertly. He crossed the grass verge to the post and held his hand out. Robert refused, afraid of dislodging the kitten and having the brothers notice it wriggling.

'Suit yersel,' he said, and picked out the kernels. He tossed the empty shells at the river, but they didn't make the water and spun across the ice. 'Dodgin school, eh? Yer faither'll gie ye a beltin.'

Brendan hunched grumpily. 'Oor faither tellt us tae get lost till teatime,' he said. 'Uncle George and Uncle Frank an wur aunties are round furra pairty. We wurnae allowed tae stay.'

'Pity,' mumbled Robert, and James eyed him suspiciously.

'Aye, it isnae fair,' Brendan went on. 'We're auld enough tae join in. Maw takes keep-money aff us. Ah'll huv tae go back an make James' tea furrim cause they'll be arguin again.'

Robert turned his head slightly to look at Brendan. He had to squint because the sun was getting low and his fine hair fell into his eyes. He saw only a huge outline, a big, silhouetted clod, and felt irritated and contemptuous.

'Well they shouldnae drink poteen then, should they? Ma faither says it makes ye go mad.'

There was silence for a second, and then Robert was knocked from the post by a hand that felt like a side of beef. James stood over him and prodded him in his stomach with a big apprentice foundry worker's boot.

'Shut up you.'

Prod.

'Ma faither isn't a fuckin Mason, is he? Ma faither says yours is. That's how yours stays workin an ma faither hus tae get the dole. Fuckin Prod.'

Prod.

'So he cannae afford the fancy stuff your faither drinks. Can he, bastart?'

He swung his boot harder, much harder. Robert tumbled over, but he was well padded against the cold, so it didn't hurt. He was more aware of the kitten's fur tickling his chin as it peeped out. Brendan gasped.

'Oh aye, whit's the wee Prod been hidin fae us then?' James lifted the kitten by its scruff and dangled it. It squealed and spat.

'Gie it back. Please.'

'Fuck off, Prod. Brendan, hold 'im. Wur gonnae play a game.'

Robert was hauled up, his arms pinned behind his back. James reached into his pocket and cracked two more walnuts, shaking the shells empty. ' 'Ve ye ever seen this? Ma faither showed me this when Ah wis wee.'

One by one, he jammed the shells over the kitten's paws, like little clogs; miraculously, they stayed on. He placed the kitten on the ice and shoved it out with his toe.

The kitten tried to stand: its legs splayed and its chin cracked down on the ice. Its back legs pistoned furiously and it collapsed again, mewling. Brendan and James laughed, their ugly ham-chop mouths wide and roaring. Robert's arm was twisted, and when he yelped he realized that he too had been laughing.

The kitten hauled itself up for one final effort. Its rear end wobbled and it upended itself, back on the ice and legs in the air.

'Jist like Charlie Chaplin!' cried James, holding his sides. He collected the kitten from the ice and shook it above his head, not too roughly. It was exhausted. Brendan let Robert go. They expected him to dance around James and plead for the kitten, so he shoved his hands in his pockets and looked at his feet

'You don't like us Fenians, dae ye?' asked James. 'We shout an swear an make whiskey outa meths. We're no respectable enough, ur we? Dae ye know whit else we dae?' He leaned down and suspended the kitten in front of Robert's eyes. 'We eat cats!'

He laughed loudly and suddenly ran off. After a second, Brendan whooped and joined him. They sprinted down the path. In the developing gloom, Robert saw a tiny shape being tossed between them.

He scuffed his way back to town, throwing stones and kicking an old billy-can he found in the gutter. He didn't regret losing the kitten, and was only troubled by a vague resentment for having something taken from him. He knew, of course, that they wouldn't eat the kitten. Cats were sometimes thrown off the railway bridge, and once he had watched some boys from the other side of town truss up the old gypsy widow's dog and throw it on a bonfire, but James and Brendan weren't like that. They would torment the kitten for a couple of days, then throw it out or give it to someone as a pet when the novelty wore off.

By the time he reached his parents' black-stone terraced house, it was dark and he was late for dinner. He dragged his feet across the threshold, hung his jacket in the hall press and handed his mother the waxy bread paper she wrapped his lunch in. She looked at him fiercely, but was serving his father and so had no time to ask him any questions.

'Bobby,' his father called. Robert looked at him, disgusted by the sweat smears down his face and the mouthful of gravy-soaked bread he spoke through. 'Ye've bin oot playin again, huvn't ye? Yer Ma's hud yer dinner oan fur ages.'

'Sorry, Da, Ah forgoat the time.'

'Aye, well, afore ye sit doon, ye can go a message. The accumulator in the radio's done. Away doon the garage an get a recharged wan. Ah want tae hear whit that bastart Hitler's up tae.'

Robert was quite happy to go, even though it was a ten minute errand: he liked the garage, with its huge pump arms suspended above the kerb. They creaked in the wind like monsters from another planet. Most of all, though, he enjoyed the smell of petrol: he had listened to radio reports of the bombing in Spain, and imagined the villages would smell like that.

The attendant exchanged the accumulators and Robert paid the halfpenny charge. He was missing his dinner and decided not to dawdle outside the lighted living room windows on the way home. His iron-shod shoes clacked on the cobbles and he tried to turn it into as quick a heel-toe rhythm as he could. He had his head down, watching his steps, as he turned to find some commotion farther down his street.

About twenty people had gathered outside the Coyle house, his parents among them. There was a hubbub of conversation and a diesel engine wheezed. As he approached, he saw an old ambulance juddering by the kerb, its doors thrown wide. He kept to the back of the crowd, peering between bodies for a better view. He could make out two stretchers inside the ambulance, pale faces above thin blankets.

He circled the group. In front of the ambulance Mr

Wise's butcher's van was parked, the big cart horse stamping and steaming impatiently in the cold, its bit jingling. It was often commandeered by the council for use as a mortuary wagon: fascinated, he could see four bundles laid out on crude wooden palettes. James stood by the big rear wheel, smoking and talking excitedly to a blue-uniformed policeman who held two small earthenware jars. Brendan crouched in the gutter, head in his hands.

His father was standing aside, talking to Mr McGuire from next door. He seemed animated, explaining something, his hands demonstrating strange processes. Robert sidled up and set the accumulator down against the wall behind his father's feet.

'Aye, Ah saw auld man Coyle daein it wance. That's how they dae it, aye. Hoat brick fae the oven, in the pan, meths ower it. Ah saw it. Went in purple, like. Came oot clear, nae poisons ur nuthin. Course, he hud tae get it jist right, or ...' he gestured at the scene.

Robert listened to his father's description and realized that he had misjudged the Coyles. They were not wild, irresponsible creatures: they were alchemists, dabbling in exotic, dangerous rituals. He listened to the whispered snatches of conversation – '... went blind ...', '... screaming ...', '... serves them right ...' – as he wormed through legs to catch sight of the house, now enlarged in his mind by the horror of what must have gone on in there. It looked no different, though: the shabby curtains, the grimy windows, the front door peeling oxblood paint, its number awry.

He stared into the darkened hallway, and a pair of yellow-green eyes, panic-stricken, blinked back at him from the bottom of the staircase.

Magicians had familiars. They were often cats.

Around him, the crowd shifted to look at the ambulance, its engine rattling as it moved away. He reacted to the crowd's distraction quickly, scurrying low across the pavement and into the house. He scooped up the kitten and fled down the hallway towards the kitchen.

'Hoi, who was that?' someone shouted behind him, but he pelted on. He was almost lost when he skidded in a pool of yellowy bile on the kitchen floor, banging his elbow painfully as he steadied himself, but he kept his feet, even managing to hurdle a fallen chair. The back door was unlocked, though he fumbled with the smooth round handle, the ceramic slippery and wet. He bolted through the door just as he heard footsteps coming along the hallway.

He scuttered across the small yard, throwing aside damp sheets hung on the washing line. Vaulting the wall, holding the kitten jubilantly towards the sky, he ran down the dark alleyway towards the river.

Dismantled

Sa belter o a mornin. Dead sunny, but. Place desertit, no a soul. Headin tae the newsagent doon Fairway Avenue, get a *Sunday Mail* n a pint o milk, mebbe some bacon n a coupla rolls fur breakfast. Feels like it should be wan o they Sundays fae years ago. You know, like nae cars, afore cars got that common, like, n the air tastit clean n everythin looked really sparklin.

Ah huvny slept n Ah'm sober, but Ah'm no feelin too good. Bit vague, like. S'jist it wis a funny night. Dead weird. Really dead, fuckin strange.

Teamed up wi Stevie n wee Iain doon Cutter's. No their local, which is jist as well cause Iain's a bit o a bampot. Still, Ah'm oan ma ownio late gettin oot n missed the boys oan their way tae Toledo, n cannae be arsed catchin them up. Besides, Stevie n Iain ur tryin tae lumber these three lassies, n they seem tae be interestit in the dark-haired wans, which suits yours truly cause Ah think they're dogs, n the other wan's sumthin else, eighteen mebbe, long blonde hair, really curly, n this dead nice smile n tits you'd die tae get yer hauns oan, but she's a bit young fur that, like, n a wee bit class n aw. Lesley. Chemistry student at the tech, she says, n she's sort o lookin at me fae under her eyelashes.

Ah'm talkin tae her aboot the garage, been there five years, n she's really listenin tae me like, so Ah tell her aboot ma Dolly Sprint Ah'm gonnae do up when Ah've goat the cash. Most folk think Fords are the biz, like Fiestas n RS2000s, but the Dolly's a beauty. Alloy heid, two litre, sixteen valve, twin SUs. Jist aboot tae ask her if she'd like tae go furra drive in it when Alex the barman, smart cunt, asks wee Iain how the wife is, looks smug then fucks off tae the other end o the bar.

'So are you married?' wan o the dogs asks. Iain says 'Aye, sorta: the wife left me.' Then he starts tellin them aboot his wife n him n how they'd agreed no tae tie each other doon n how he felt trapped, like, if he couldnae go oot wi the boys n everythin like that, n Lesley goes aw stiff n the bird Stevie's been chattin up asks whose idea that arrangement wis, his or hers. He says whit difference dis that make n she jist tuts, so he goes, 'You wan o these feminist cunts, like?' n they aw breathe in, sharpish. Ah feel dead uncomfy cause Ah wis gettin oan awright wi Lesley n Ah'm no usually cheeky tae women, like, but Ah laugh tae try tae make a joke o it. They pick up their haunbags dead quick n go tae the bog n Ah hear wan o them say, 'Dickheids' as they go past. Stevie says, 'They're off. Frigid cunts,' then shouts, 'Fuckin lezzies,' after them, n Iain goes mental at Alex, callin him a fuckin twistit big bastart, but Alex isnae jist big, he's fuckin huge n threatens tae kick Iain's arse ootside n bar him, n Iain shuts up then, but he says he's gonnae chib him, by the way, n he's fuckin fizzin fur the rest o the night.

Right enough, eftir fifteen minutes they're no back n they must've legged it oot the fire door. Stevie says that's it, end o story, n he husnae had his hole fur three weeks since he finished wi that wee bird fae Cadbury's n he's been oan night shift. Iain says we're stuck cause we've missed the curfew n last orders is aboot tae go so we get a triple in, me wi a pint n a double voddy which is guaranteed tae finish me aff. Stevie's gaun roon tae Iain's cause he says he's goat hauf a case o super lagers, n Iain says tae me why don't Ah come cause he's goat some acid tabs Ah could gie a go n Stevie grins like. Never tried acid, jist some hash n a snowbaw at a rave wance but Ah don't like tae show it, so Ah say awright, that's the gemme, n Alex says 'Good night, Iain,' as wur going oot, sarky like, n Iain, dead cool, jist sticks up his middle finger wioot even turnin roon.

We're oot, n it's a bit breezy. Iain lives in the cooncil flats up the back o the scheme, aboot hauf n oor's walk. Stevie's got a quarter bottle o Whyte n Mackays, n we take slugs oot o that oan the way. Iain's fuckin mental, lobs a coupla bricks at the hole-in-the-waw at Safeways, cracks them at it really hard, but the screen's doon n they jist bounce aff. The scheme's okay, jist a panda car cruises a coupla times, n Iain's cold, fuckin iceman, like they wurnae even there, n they see his face n mebbe they know him n mebbe they don't but they don't fancy messin, n Ah don't fuckin blame them.

Iain's fuckin furious when we get back tae the flats cause some cat's been pissin in the stairwell n it's fuckin stinkin. I will tell them it minds me o a book Ah read at school, some borin junk aboot a guy n screens in the waw that watched him n some bird he tortured. The flats he lived in smellt o boiled cabbage n ma teacher made a big thing aboot how this description wis dead good, n Iain jist says 'Oh aye?' – opens the door.

His wee lassie's up oan her own, watchin Hunter oan the telly. She's aboot thirteen, wi short dark hair n these big brown eyes, n she's still wearin her school claes. 'This is Melanie,' Iain says, n she smiles n goes, 'Hi,' but he disnae tell her ma name n she seems tae know Stevie already.

At first Ah think the flat's no bad cause there's curtains tae match the three-piece suite n a budgie cage n a spankin telly n video, but it's a fuckin coup by the way, cause there's ashtrays everywhere n chip wrappers in a bin n this fruit bowl wi wan scabby auld apple n a mucky knife. The wee lassie hus tae get up tae gie me a seat so she starts tae feed the budgie, n Iain n Stevie shift claes aff the settee. Iain asks me if Ah want anything tae eat, but ma stomach couldnae staun it so Ah say naw, n him n Stevie go tae the kitchen tae make cheese n toast. Ah staun aside the lassie n talk tae the budgie, a fat blue thing, but Ah'm no too steady oan ma feet. Ah make wee suckin noises n click ma tongue, but it jist looks at me as if Ah wis a fuckin idiot. So Ah says, 'S'no very friendly,' n she says they used tae huv a pair, but the female died n Billy's been pinin since. Ah look at it n Ah cannae tell if it's a boy or a lassie, so Ah say, 'How can ye tell?' She looks at me like Ah'm stupit, but nice, like Ah'm her wee brother, n says, 'Everybody knows that,' n Ah don't want tae look a tube so Ah says, 'Aw, right,' like Ah've jist minded, n Ah think Ah do know, but Ah've furgoatten, like.

Ah sit in wan o the chairs n try tae watch the telly,

but Ah cannae follow it cause Ah'm too fuckin pished, the words dinnae make any sense. Iain n Stevie come back in eatin these saggy bits o toast, n Stevie gies me a can o super lager. Ah reckon Ah'd better drink it slow, like, but Iain n Stevie huv two each, n Iain gets oot the tabs. He gies me wan, stauns there haudin it oot until Ah take it n looks at me as if Ah'd better. Ah take it n swallow n it catches in ma throat so Ah wash it doon wi some super lager, n Ah say ur they huvin wan but Stevie says naw, they're gonnae skin up n Ah wish Ah knew that afore cause Ah'm shittin it. Iain sits doon n tells the wee lassie tae sit oan the couch tween him n Stevie.

Ah'm fuckin wrecked, by the way, like ma neck cannae haud ma fuckin heid up n Ah hope Ah'm gonnae spew ma load so's Ah can get rid o the fuckin tab, but Iain wid likely kick ma teeth in fur wastin it so Ah jist sit there. The room's fuckin dancin, like the telly's hauf way across the fuckin ceiling. There's music cause the programme's finished, n then adverts, n mair music, n mair adverts, n Ah huvnae a fuckin clue.

N Ah cannae follow anything, cannae even haud a conversation. Iain looks at me like Ah'm fuckin dirt n says Ah'm wastit n Stevie says aye, n caws me a spawny wee shite n Ah should be home wi ma Maw, but they're jist takin the pish, like. Ah try tae watch them, n Stevie leans his heid back n finishes his smoke, dead relaxed, n Iain hus his arm roon wee Melanie n he's strokin her hair. He says sumthin in her ear, but she shakes her heid n he says, 'Dae as yer tellt.' Stevie looks at him n says, 'Ur we oan?', n Iain says aye, they are, n sort o pushes the wee lassie up ontae her feet n says, 'Aren't we darlin?' Ah try tae say sumthin, but Ah don't know whit, n this lump o puke comes up the back o ma throat n Ah huv tae swallow n breathe deep n blow hard tae keep it doon. The three o them go oot, n Ah laugh a bit cause wee Melanie looks jist like ma pal did when he wis up in court fur breakin n enterin, dead wee tween these two polis that wur like fuckin bears. Iain goes, 'Jist let yersel oot when yer ready, son,' n Ah jist aboot manage tae say aye, thanks.

So Ah'm oan ma ownio again, but Ah couldnae gie a shit cause Ah'm ready fur the fuckin knacker's yard. Ma heid's fuckin burstin n Ah've goat tae get some fresh air, but ma legs willnae work, the bastarts, n ma eyes ur gettin dead heavy n Ah'm thinkin Ah might be able tae sleep it aff. Then the fuckin tab hits me, don't know what the fuck's goin oan. There's this zap, bright light jist furra second n this rush, like n electric breeze past ma ear, n the room's glowin, like a million candles.

Ah close ma eyes, try tae make it go away, but when Ah open them it husnae changed, n there's this lassie's face oan the telly, n it's streamin oot light, n it starts tae change n she begins tae step oota the telly, climbin oot, n then the wee lassie's staunin in the middle o the room. It's her that's glowin, no exactly her, s'hard tae explain, but she's charged, static like, n these wee points o light, fuckin hunners n thoosans, stickin tae her, like she's crustit wi these wee luminous pearls, n she turns her heid n looks at me through them n smiles n her mooth is rid, really rid like rubies, n you cannae see her teeth, jist this rid, rid slash through aw this whiteness.

She walks across the room, fuckin blows ma mind cause she leaves this trail eftir hur, like shadows or ghosts or photographs, like where she's jist been left behind furra second. She goes tae the fruit bowl n picks up the knife: Ah shits masel thinkin what she's gonnae dae cause Ah still cannae move n Ah reckon Ah'm furrit. But she goes fur the budgie cage, lookin at me aw the time wi that fuckin mad grin, n she opens the door n reachs in. Ah'm tryin tae tell the budgie tae move itself, fuckin daft bird, but it jist sits there. It disnae struggle but Ah can hear it cheepin, jist this faint wee squawk, n it looks so fuckin weird, blue feathers against aw those glitterin points o light, like it's the only fuckin thing in the whole room Ah can recognize n that makes it look like sumthin fae another fuckin planet.

She brings it ower tae me. It's in her haun, its wee neckless heid lookin up at her n you could have sworn they knew each other, that they were playin some gemme they'd played furra thoosan fuckin years. She lays it doon oan the flair right at ma feet, n Ah'm tryin tae say, look, Ah don't want it hen, thanks aw the same, but Ah still cannae speak n it jist lies there, wee feet in the air, quiet, n she takes wan wing n spreads it oot, n it's fuckin huge, really long like a fuckin eagle's, n pins it wi her left knee, then takes the other wan, pins it wi her right. Ah'm fuckin squirmin inside, n she looks up at me n she knows Ah don't want tae see, n that rid mooth o hers says 'Watch,' n her voice is slow n deep n there's a whisper o an echo n Ah cannae look away.

She takes the knife n puts the point at the budgie's throat, n it's still makin this cheepin noise, even when the point slips in n makes this wee horizontal cut. Then she swivels it, draws it right doon its belly, n it's still alive, it's still chirpin away like it's fuckin talkin tae her, n she takes the two wee corners at its throat, n peels them apart, n there's this sound like when you rip a bit o wet chamois. She folds the skin back n there's some kind o fluid, but Ah cannae see any guts, like its stomach or nuthin. She bends ower it, sort o sniffin, n she pokes the knife in n tugs it oot. A wee wire comes oot oan the point, dead thin wi green n yellow insulation, n she has tae turn the knife edge oan n snap it n there's this wee spark.

Then she reaches in wi her fingers, pullin wan end o the wire, n the stuff inside sort o moves a bit n a wee square chip comes oot, shinin sort o purply n bluey-green, like dragonflies' wings. A wee drop clings tae wan corner, n Ah think it's blood, but then Ah see a point o light reflecting in its surface, n I've seen reflections like that afore, practically every fuckin day, man, n it's oil. She pulls the other end o the wire n a wee cog comes oot, n she looks at me n smiles, n Ah smile too cause it's okay, n the wee toy budgie's still chirpin, n Ah know it's tellin her tae carry oan, it's aw part o the game.

But then she takes the knife, like, n she dangles it above the budgie's heid, n grins, but different, n the wee thing starts fuckin squealin, like really fuckin screamin its fuckin heid aff, n Ah try tae tell her no tae dae whatever the fuck she's gonnae dae, n Ah think she's gonnae poke its eyes oot, but the point o the knife goes in the wee blue fleshy bit, jist above its beak, n the noise is terrible. She starts tae pull the wee blue bit aff, it's like a nail comin away fae yer finger, n there's wee bloody fibres stickin tae the beak. The bird is pure screamin fur mercy, but she tears away n it comes right aff oantae the point o the knife n it wriggles there n wee splashes o blood drip oantae the lights aroon her fingers.

'This is the only bit that's real: everybody knows that,' she says, n she looks at it n puts her tongue oot n jist tastes it. Then she laughs n says 'Blue furra boy'' n flicks it aff the knife n it lands oan ma shirt. Ah look doon at it n there's this patch o blood, gettin bigger n bigger, n the fuckin thing starts movin, crawlin up ma shirt. Ah'm no fur that fuckin thing touchin ma skin, but Ah cannae move, n Ah cannae say anything, n even if Ah could naebody would hear ower the sound o her laughin n the fuckin noise the budgie's makin.

N then it's ower. Just like that, Ah come to. It's well light, n Ah'm sittin in the chair, hauns grippin the arms, n Ah'm sweatin like a pig. The lassie's no there n the telly's still oan, adverts fur joabs, n Ah look doon at ma shirt n it's clean, nae blood. Ah move ma fingers, then ma feet, then rub ma face n hope tae fuck what they say aboot flashbacks isnae true. There's a pink frilly cover ower the budgie cage, but Ah'll be fucked if Ah'm lookin under it.

The whole situation's mental, like, so Ah decide tae get the fuck oot, but Ah cannae find Iain. He's no in the kitchen n there's a door tae a bedroom lyin open wi a double bed n a heap o shite aw ower the place, socks n trainers n Ys, but nae Iain. There's a door closed, wi a wee tile oan it, red poppies roon the edge n 'Melanie's Room' in fancy letters, n Ah can hear noise, movement like. Ah knock it n there's a cough fae inside n the noise stops. The door opens a wee bit n Iain looks oot n he's aw bleary eyed n he rubs his haun ower his chin n his heid n he disnae look at ma face. 'Fuck's sake', he says, 'you still here.'

'Aye,' Ah says, 'Ah must've fell asleep. Ah'm jist going.'

'Aye, well, see ye later, big man,' he says, n he goes

tae close the door.

'Is Stevie in there?' Ah ask.

N He looks at me, right in ma eyes now, n he says, 'Whit the fuck has that goat tae do wi' you? Fuck off.'

So Ah says, 'Awright. Nae offence,' but there's a wee dressin table wi a mirror behind him, n Ah can jist make oot a shape sittin oan the edge o a bed n the wee lassie lyin doon n she's lookin right at me in the reflection n she opens her mooth tae say sumthin n then shuts it n Ah jist smile n Ah know it's aw wrang, like.

Iain says, 'Aye, right. See ye,' n shuts the door, n Ah jist leave. Ah close the front door quiet n stand ootside furra minute, n Ah don't reckon Ah will see them cause they're bad news. Better tae avoid them.

Sa belter o a mornin, but. Ah'm feelin a bit spaced oot, bit empty, like. Ah reckon at first it's jist the booze n the tab, but Ah cannae shake it. Ah sit doon oan the grass ootside the newsagent n drink a can o Pepsi.

The *Mail's* jist the same as alweys. Some guy gonnae get hung in Turkey. Serbs rapin women again. Gazza's finest hour. The 'tic slip up, need furra big name striker. In a wee column cawd 'World news', there's a fuzzy wee photie o some postman fae Texas that took a gun tae his workmates, killt four o them, n he looks like ma maw's milkman. It's aw the fuckin same, alweys will be. It's no like me, but Ah feel dead pissed off, like really, really fucked off wi everything, no jist fitba, no jist mair fuckin horror stories fae fuckin Kosovo. It's mair than that.

Then Ah mind that lassie fae last night. Lesley. She wis dead nice. Nice smile. Chemistry student. At the tech. Should be able tae track her doon, maybe ask her tae the pictures, decent, like.

Christ, Ah've gottae dae sumthin.

Gifts

I. Blue Note

It was *Silence of the Lambs*, of course. He recognized it straight away. There was that throb, that timpanic thrum that reverberated deep in his gut. Basement rooms, dimly lit. Walls, bare rough plaster. He was looking for someone, and he knew who it was but couldn't name them. Or it. Bare light bulbs swung overhead, perhaps the opening credits of *Callan*: he could be very creative. Eclectic. Nothing was out of hand. Not yet.

He even knew the rooms. The clutter of beds and armchairs and the striped beige wallpaper. Fusty old bedspreads and tapestries. Huge porcelain ewers. The old flat from Clouston Street, the first place he and Heather had together, but laid out completely differently, of course. And filled with things they'd never owned. But their flat. And because he knew it, he knew where the danger would come from, and he could anticipate it.

He held his gun out, though naturally it would never fire – he had already dismissed calling for help on the telephone, since that would simply be another frustration – but it made him feel better. He pointed it to his left, knowing the danger would then come from the right. He waited. It came closer, from behind him as he expected. He felt it scurrying along the floor, under the legs of chairs, swishing under bed covers which draped long onto the threadbare red carpet. It was time to do something. Attract attention.

He began to howl. Quietly at first, the breath coming out as a whimper, but he'd left enough time. It was easy, he'd had lots of practice. He imagined himself deep under water, very dark, and he had to shriek himself to the surface, and the scene would disappear and he would come up for air.

He knew he was getting louder. The water was

thick – perhaps he was buried – but he would get there, he would, if he kept going, kept howling like a dog. All he had to do was get his eyes open and he'd be there, back in the air, all he had to do was keep howling and

'Graham. Graham. Wake up.'

Good. He hated waking alone. It was better if someone heard him, held out a hand to drag him up, out.

'Graham. Wake up. You're having a nightmare. Wake up quick.'

Heather. Back. Bless her.

'Graham. Quick.'

He opened his eyes. Yeah. As ever, he felt a rush of affection, even love, and Heather made up for all the things she had and hadn't done to him with this one simple act of waking him up when he needed her most.

'Graham. Quick. Something's wrong. Call an ambulance.'

Oh fuck, he thought, oh fuck. What's happened? Wrists, knives from the kitchen? Pills, maybe, or …

'Look,' and her hand went to her cheek and her nails bit deep and the flesh fell away black and glutinous from her face and her eyeball slipped and she looked so sad and helpless and reached out to him with a handful of

he hit the roof, woke up cursing jesus fucking shite bastard in mid air and that was it. He was breathing hard and lashing sweat and he felt hunted, just in case, just in case his bastarding psyche was doing it again and this still wasn't reality. Christ, the nightmares were bad enough, but when he decided to play this dirty trick on himself, he knew he wasn't getting any sleep that night, or the next, or the next.

He collapsed onto the pillow, turned over, clicked on the bedside lamp and flipped open the top of his cigarette packet. His hands were shaking, and he spilled the half dozen cigarettes inside. He picked one, shoved the rest back and brushed a few crumbs of loose tobacco off the duvet cover. The filter tasted of wet chalk. He struck his lighter a few times. It eventually managed a weak blue flame, and he lit up, then put out the light to concentrate on the sound of his smoking: kiss-suck, the frazzle of burning tobacco, kiss-suck. It was a comforting sound. If you needed to listen.

Throwing back the covers, he swung out of bed and shoved his feet into his slippers. There wasn't any point in trying to get back to sleep, he'd only slip into yet another fucking nightmare. The flat was warm – white-meter heating uselessly burning up money in the middle of night, maybe that had made him uncomfortable while he slept – so he didn't bother with a dressing gown. Neither did he put on any lights, preferring the dark.

He had a choice. In the bathroom, a tiny bottle of red and white capsules; in the kitchen, a half bottle of vodka. Mutually exclusive, the doctor'd said. So he rinsed a dirty glass and dug out the carton of orange juice from the fridge. Then, ashtray, cigarettes, lighter, vodka, juice and glass balanced along his forearm, he kicked open the drawing room door.

Lucozade-coloured streetlight convulsed across the walls and ceiling, filtering through the branches and leaves of the tree growing a few feet from the front window. He clicked on a lamp, enough of a yellow glow to choose a record by. Art Blakey. Ideal for a miserable mood. He flipped up the cover of the record deck, flicked on the amplifier and selected a track. He loved watching the glow of the valve amp in the dark, the music washing out from a Manhattan skyline.

He curled up in the bay window seat, leaning his forehead against the cold glass, nursing the knot in the pit of his stomach. Outside, a blind man edged along the pavement, white stick scraping the kerb edge. A taxi approached from one end of the street, little orange light on; from the opposite direction, a man peered out into the road, began to raise his hand to hail it. Graham lowered his head and breathed deep into his chest.

He closed his eyes and wished he could be with Heather. Ten years together was too long. He missed her so much he'd got sick of missing her. He'd tired of playing the old game when he couldn't be with her: lying still and imagining her face and superimposing it on his own so that her features became his and he smiled and frowned and pouted the way she did. If she was here, she would fold herself around him and ease the blackness. But if she was here, he wouldn't have got the blackness in the first place.

The taxi scuttled down the street, rattling away like a half-empty biscuit tin. He imagined it bringing Heather back home. Then there was another sound, like static, rising above it all. He tried to open his eyes but couldn't.

A white light flashed, more intense than headlights. Burning red blotches appeared on the inside of his eyelid, twisting, turning indigo. He heard a car horn.

His head jerked up, confused by what he hadn't seen through the window. For the smallest moment, he saw a wash of silver gush down the street, like mercury running along the pavement, over the taxi in mid-swerve, to the kerb, the blind-man and the pedestrian, up walls, so quickly racing over roofs and away, disappearing into thin air. He drew his breath in: his hands were around his knees, and he noticed the remains of a luminescence, evaporating like marsh gas from his fingertips.

Something had happened; the taxi was slewed across the pavement, the contents of a litter bin strewn around it. The pedestrian was kneeling, running his hand along the white line, looking down the length of the street in both directions. It sounded like he was shouting something, but Graham couldn't hear through the window. The blind man looked perplexed, reaching out as if he was trying to catch a butterfly suspended in front of his face.

A faint mist blew off down the street. There wasn't another car around to explain the accident. A motorbike would have moved fast enough, but he hadn't heard anything. Maybe the taxi driver was drunk. And Graham could've dozed off, just for a second, enough to invent a new little quirk for the night-time heebie-jeebies.

But he wasn't so sure. The men outside weren't behaving like ordinary witnesses. Then again, they weren't were they? A blind man and a loony. Not much there for the police to get into. And there hadn't been any movement from the taxi. The driver could be hurt. Dead. He should dial 999, he supposed, but it wasn't his problem. Besides, he hadn't really seen anything, and lights were going on in the flats across the street. Someone else would do it.

Heather would have.

He downed his vodka, poured another. The record finished, the arm sliding across the groove and ending in a gentle pss-ptt, pss-ptt. He left it.

The drawing room door opened and he started. A head poked through.

'Graham. I heard a noise in the street. Then the music. Are you okay?'

'Yeah. Sorry. You made me jump: I thought you were Heather.'

'Nope. Just your resident hanger-on. Hey, is there something going on out there?'

A blue light was flashing. Iain came over to the window and looked out. A policeman was talking to the blind man while another helped a woman out of the back of a taxi, a man in a short-sleeved shirt looking on. 'Has there been an accident? Did you see anything?'

'Not really. Something bright.' He looked up at Iain, the long hair receding on his forehead, the angular nose, the look of complete self-confidence. Just before Heather had left, Graham had found one of Iain's socks under the wicker chair in their bedroom. Mislaid, gathered up in the wrong washing pile, she'd said. 'I don't know.'

'Drama, eh? So what's up? Could you not sleep?'

'You ask a lot of questions for a mere lodger, Iain.'

'Fuck lodger. Two and a half years we've been playing in the same bands and all you think of me is a lodger.

You're a cheeky bastard. And you can't play the trumpet to save yourself.'

Graham laughed. 'Two and a half years of you pissing off nine months out of twelve on your pan-European travels. The band's managed fine without you.'

'Yeah, with plooky wee stand-ins. The audiences just hang on waiting for me to come back.'

'I know. Listen. I don't want to be rude, but could you leave me alone for a while? I'm not feeling too good.'

'Aye. You're looking pale. What's up?'

'Can you not just go away?'

'No. Pals are meant to be a pain in the arse. What's wrong?'

He pressed his knuckles into the bridge of his nose, then the corners of his eyes. 'I had a nightmare. I can't get back to sleep straight away. I just need to relax a bit.'

Iain sat on one of the armchairs. 'Really? A nightmare? Fuck, I haven't had a nightmare since I was a wee boy.'

'You haven't got a brain.'

'Do you get them a lot? No really, I'm interested.'

'Sometimes. When I'm alone.'

'What was it about?'

'Heather. Well. At the end. Before that, the usual. Something out to get me. I never know what, so don't ask'

'Christ. I never knew that about you.'

'You weren't that much of a pal.'

'Thanks. No, but I wouldn't have guessed you were that – unstable. Crazy Bobby from The Halt, maybe. Harry and Mick, definitely. But I thought you were the controlled type.'

'Not the sort to get the screaming ab-dabs like a kiddie, eh?'

'Nope.'

'Well, it's part of other things. Things about the way I feel. I'm not as bad as I used to be.'

'Listen. Can I get a drink?'

There would be no losing him: he was awake and gabby and totally insensitive to Graham's need for peace. He'd have to make do with time alone later. He told him to help himself. Iain went out and came back with a glass, pouring a large, straight measure.

'So. This thing you get. Nightmares. You say they're better.'

'Yeah. I control it. It's a matter of recognizing you're dreaming and then making choices inside the dream. You can't stop it happening, but you can change it, sort of.'

'I've heard about that. How you can direct your dreams, and you remember them really clearly.'

'That's slightly different. A proper technique. I've just learned something like it for myself. Out of survival.'

'How do you do it?'

'Och, it depends. You know. I come to a door, and I know I'm going to open it, and I know that what's behind it is going to scare the shit out of me, so that gives me some sort of power. Or I'm under threat, and I can manipulate it so that I become the thing or the person that's doing the threatening for a crucial moment, so that I'm not the target. Usually, it just means that I know when to scream blue fucking murder to get myself out.'

'That's brilliant. How long did it take you to be able to do that?'

'Years. It used to be really bad.'

'How?'

'Look, I'm tired. This isn't a good topic of conversation.'

'Aw come on, it's interesting. Look on it as therapy.'

'Aye, that's what the shrink in my teens said, talking is excellent therapy.'

'There you go.'

'I don't think he had a thirty-four-year-old itinerant sax player with an ego and a pony tail in mind.' Especially one who might, perhaps, have fucked his wife.

'There's nothing wrong with my pony tail. Women

love it. So. How bad did it used to be?'

'Well ... just sometimes ... sometimes I'd feel something in the room with me.'

'Aye. Well?'

'Och, like, you know. Something after me again.'

'So what was worse about it? Come on. Spit it out.' He perked up, a flash of insight. 'Did you know what it was then?

'Yeah. It was ... sexual. Like a succubus. Or incubus.'

'Wow. Which?'

He smiled at the stupidity of it. 'Both actually, now you come to mention it.'

'Fuck's sake. What are you on about?'

Graham leaned back and looked at the ceiling, trying to grasp it, feel it again. Way up in the corner, right up in the cornicing, a smudge of pale, luminescent grey caught his eye. He'd have to dust for cobwebs. 'Sometimes I'd feel something heavy sitting on the bed, the mattress sinking at the edge. Everything was the way it should be, not like other nightmares, where I know the place but it's all changed. Then hands'd move over the bed. It climbed on my back once. I had this panic that I was going to be buggered. It leaned on my shoulders and pressed down, then released me, then down again. I could taste the pillow in my face. It kept doing it, more and more violently, bouncing me up and down. It wanted me on my back, you see. It wanted to castrate me, I think. Sometimes I still feel those hands on my shoulders. I used to be careful about not sleeping on my back, but another time it caught me. It crawled over the mattress and straddled me. I reached down to feel what it was: it was female, but greasy and animal. Everything else about it felt male: the smell, the strength, the breathing. My hand was pushed away and it lowered itself onto me and fucked me until I managed to drag myself awake.'

He gulped at his drink, his throat dry and constricted. In the silence, Iain lifted the stylus off the record, then topped up his glass.

'D'you know, I honestly thought I'd been used by something to impregnate it. It seemed real. Even years later.'

'Christ. I hate to say this, but you're off your head.'

'No. Not really. Just the occasional demon pops its head up, that's all. I'm clinically depressive. No doubt coupled with subconscious feelings of sexual inadequacy and ambivalence and a highly overactive imagination.' He turned to the window. 'Things were fine after I met Heather. She scared the bogey men and women away.'

'She never said.'

'Was there any reason why she should?'

'No. I don't suppose so.' He swilled his drink around. 'Do you miss her?'

'Of course I do. Stupid question. Sometimes I don't know why I bother going on. There's not much point without her. Do you think I want to be some sad old git who plays John Fucking Coltrane all the time and tries to get off with the young things after a gig for the sake of a quickie to stave off the boredom? Christ, Iain, you're insensitive enough to've been a drummer.'

Iain held his hands up. 'Okay. Sorry. She might come back though.'

'No. I know who she's with. He's well adjusted. I'm fucked up. Which fucked her up. She'll be very happy with him.'

'It doesn't work like that. There's no accounting for taste,' Iain said. Graham snorted. 'You know what I mean. Fuck's sake, there's more to life. Heather knows that. Look, if I did what was best for me, I'd be married to some House of Fraser freak with bleached hair, and we'd be living in Milngavie and she'd take the BMW and the weans shopping on Saturday mornings.'

'And look how you've ended up.'

'Oh yeah, smart arse. Kick a man when he's down. Except I'm not. I do as I please. My bit of writing, my bit of recording. The odd gig, except Tommy Smith's a fucking sight better than me so he got there first and I don't begrudge him. Friends help me. Like you and Heather. Do you know what it's like, having the freedom of staying with people you want to, without being tied to them? Just for the hell of it and a fucking good party. And then you move on, Edinburgh, Manchester, London, Paris and back again. It's all right, don't knock it. You move on. And if it's not Heather, if she decides she wants Milngavie and a BMW, then someone else is just around the corner. That's all right. Fuck who you want to, Graham. As long as they want to fuck you, you can't go wrong.'

'Have you, Iain?'

'Have I what?'

'Fucked who you wanted to? And did they want to back?' Was that panic in his eyes, just the briefest moment?

'Don't get paranoid as well, pal.'

'Just a question. Nothing meant.'

Iain stood up. He leaned towards him slightly. 'Why did she leave, Graham?'

'That's none of your business.'

'It is if you're accusing me of something.'

'Who said I was accusing you?'

'I say. You're accusing me of shagging your wife.'

'I'm not. I never said that.'

'You are. You did.'

'Please yourself.'

'Will I tell you something? How long has she been away? Ten weeks? Well, I hope she's enjoyed it, because you were making her life hell before she went.'

'What do you know about it?'

'More than you. The walls in here aren't that thick. And before Christmas, I came back here for lunch before afternoon rehearsals. Heather wasn't here. I made a sandwich, had a coffee. She came back from shopping. And do you know what she did? Do you?'

'You're going to tell me.'

'Aye, fucking right. She took the milk bottle and

topped it up with water. I asked her why. She burst out crying. Said you'd been looking at the levels of the bottles – the vodka, the milk, the wine – making sure no-one had been here with her during the day. I live here, I said. She said you wouldn't like it. She was worried about the loaf of bread too, just in case you had the slices counted.'

Graham didn't know she'd noticed. He'd tried to look at the bottles surreptitiously, hadn't wanted to accuse her. Christ, it was a sickness, she knew that. He trusted her: just, something in him made him need to be sure.

Like following her.

Had she noticed that too?

He turned to the window again. A tow truck had arrived, crazy orange flashers dancing on the roof of the cab. The taxi was being hooked up to the hoist at the back.

'She's taken an interdict out against me,' he said.

'Does that not tell you something then?' Iain went to the door and opened it. 'You know, Graham, you really need your head looked into.' Then he left, closing the door gently behind him.

He uncoiled himself from his seat after one more drink. He needed air, but people had gathered around the accident and he didn't fancy company. He went to the hall – Iain's light was out, the space under his door dark – and lifted his coat from the hall stand. He reached under the small bench and lifted his cornet, then decided where to go.

He hooked down the hatch to the loft, the ladders falling easily. The previous owners had floored the attic space and walled it off, intending some conversion, but they'd had to move and Graham and Heather hadn't decided what to do with it yet. Perhaps they should put intrusive lodgers up there.

Except the plural didn't sound right any more.

He climbed, wrapping the coat around him, and felt along the flooring to the skylight. A quick push with his shoulder, a squeal of rust, and it was open.

The wind had settled down to a stiff breeze and, up

on the roof, eighty feet from the ground, he should have been freezing. But he wasn't. Vodka. Probably.

His lips pursed as he raised the mouthpiece. Briefly, the image of a dog howling out his loneliness to the night came to mind, but he laughed at himself, stupid fucked-up fool trying to be romantic. Still, he filled his lungs and decided on a B♭ for effect.

It burst out, loud, vibrating like a foghorn, and went rolling out over the city. He was stunned by the volume, had meant mezzo-piano at the worst. Christ, the neighbours would be complaining. Again. In the street, the mad ambers were still dancing, and the hydraulics of the lift drowned out the sound of voices, but there was no way they couldn't have heard him. Not that loud. Shit.

Still, no lights went on in the dark attic flats opposite. There was one light showing, but it had been since he'd come up: he watched the yellow curtains to see if there was a twitch, and if he hadn't, he wouldn't have seen it coming.

It seemed to simply trundle across his line of sight, obscuring the window for a second. His eyes followed it, and it was coming nearer.

A sphere, a deep, deep blue, night-navy, but across its surface, it shimmered, palely silver, tiny grains of watery light winking.

It was coming nearer. And it was getting louder.

Graham couldn't move. It still came on, heading directly for him. It didn't seem solid, but he closed his eyes and waited for some kind of impact.

It came. Water. Cold water seemed to be pouring into him through his chest. He felt something bleed from him, and an ache settled in his joints and bones. Through the sound, he was aware of being somewhere else.

With Heather.

Her perfume, CKone, her latest, filled his head, and her hair smelled of apples and coconut and it was rich and smooth and stroked her back, her bare back and over her shoulders and down, hanging in space, and it moved and tickled and she gasped and flung herself back as she rode something, and she was gripped around her waist, slim and sweating she rode something which filled up her cunt and she skewered herself down, harder, harder

Fuck. Fuck. Fuck.

Fuck

his spine arched. A warmth grew, and a sensation he'd never experienced before exploded in him, coursing along his veins, silvering the inside of his skin.

Graham fought to catch his breath. He couldn't see, and his ears were filled with the noise, the sound of the B♭ come back to him, playing pure and clear and blue around his skull.

Oh no.

Please no.

He'd wished he could be with Heather.

II. Filament

Can you give me a second? I still haven't quite got the hang of it.

Let me just

just

That's it.

Aye, I did see something. I did. Not through my eyes. My optic nerves withered away after the disease. Whatever it is that's happened, whatever it is that's left behind, I'm positive I didn't get any stimulation through my eyes.

You see ... Christ, I can't believe how often I still say that. I'll start again.

Look, being blind is really inconvenient. I'm not being funny. Not knowing where you are and how your environment pans out in front of you. All you can be sure about is the space you take up, your flesh and blood and bone. Everything outside what you can touch is ... unknown. A micron's distance might as well be a light year. And every movement becomes a test of nerve, or a test of faith: you have to believe that the void you're stepping into is unoccupied, it's not going to be taken up by another human being, or a car, or a wild animal.

Still, faith isn't such a bad thing, I suppose.

But what I've found real trouble coping with is what was inside my head. Maybe it's just me. Maybe everyone reacts differently when their sight's taken away. I found things slipping, memories wasting because – I don't know – maybe the frame of reference I used to measure the past or the present or the future was gone.

I'm probably not making myself clear. It's as if your mind's ... given validity for thinking in visual terms because there are visual images out there. In reality. And when reality's gone, what basis is there for the pictures you've got in your head? I'll tell you what happened.

At the beginning, it was like a thousand images blowing about in my head

my big brother and his wife and two children children

the picture of my mum and dad
on their first date at London Zoo

where I processed loan applications

 and 

out my granny's back door when I helped her do the gardening on summers' days

Tony Benn

tortoiseshell cats
going over the Forth Bridge
red bow ties

sledge runners slashing wounds in snowy hillsides
sledge runners slashing wounds in snowy hillsides

NEON LIGHTS

above the old Odeon cinema
in Pollokshaws
gold candles in brushed brass holders
the test card

&

Celtic and Dunfermline
football
strips

my da's old ***Humber Sceptre***
pink seashells

mustard coloured polystyrene hamburger cartons

the King of ♦monds

school ties chrome
bumpers chameleons,

no wait ***Please***

an ex-girlfriend dancing the tango with her pal, black hair swept over her bare shoulders and black satin dress, her smile like a snarl of sexuality that melted my heart and made me desperate to be inside her at the same time

imagine watching that every day, whipping past, your life chucked away on hurricanes blowing from the Irish sea over the Galloway cliffs into a sky the colour of bruised peach and granite

and you try your hardest to catch them, dance after them, capering about like a maddie, holding stuffed armfuls that slip and scurry away

or they've got minds of their own and they pirouette out of reach just when you think you've got one cornered ...

imagine

a head full of litter, dead leaves, discarded photographs, swirling about, sapping your sanity every single day.

Then that happened. That night.

See, I'd gone for a walk. I'd been restless all evening: Saturday night television's even more crap for me than for you. So I went for a walk. At 3 am? Why not? You see things differently. Pun intended. You think the dark's more dangerous, footsteps behind you, alleyways hiding you can't tell what, crowds of drunken yobs hanging round the kebab shop doorway. And I agree. It's not safe for a lot of vulnerable people, and I should imagine you'd feel that way. But remember, it's always dark for me. Think of the dangers that *aren't* around at that time in the morning. No traffic. No bargain hunters with umbrellas. No slippery-fingered hardhats up on scaffolding waiting to drop a spanner on my works. No conscientious citizens, no Boy Scouts out to bag a badge.

And I was enjoying it. It was really quiet, and cold. Of course, I heard the taxi coming a long way off. I love taxis, they've got this totally unique noise. It sounds like a machine determined to rattle itself apart from the inside, shedding nuts and bolts and gaskets until all that's left is some suicidal little cylinder quaking in a puddle of oil.

I know. I get carried away.

The taxi passed me, going south. Then there was a noise. Not a loud noise, not unpleasant. And difficult to describe. Something like ... a sigh. Or

Ahh – whofffff. That's it. Ahh – whofffff. Like a rush of air. Nothing more.

I heard the taxi swerving, tyres squealing. It hit the kerb and then crashed through something concrete on the pavement. Somebody said later it was a litter bin, but I couldn't tell at the time. I wasn't really paying attention to what happened after the sigh: I heard somebody calling out some women's names, I think, and a bit later I might have heard a trumpet note.

But, all sorts of things were happening in my head. First of all, there was this huge spotlight. No. More like ... a lighthouse lens, know what I mean? Glass. Thick. Brilliant, shimmering, really, really bright. It was sore. Concentric circles. Then, it starts unravelling, in one piece, one coil, really thin. Like apple peel. Much more fragile, though. It just pulls itself apart, stretches itself out for miles – no, not miles – years. Decades. A spiral of light. I remember light, but this is more than just a memory of light. I used to think the memory of things was better than reality. Not this, though. This is glorious.

It just hangs there, in the blackness inside my head. It's delicate and immensely strong, quivering slightly, like a cobweb filament. And what I'm finding is, all the scraps inside my head, all the crazy memories, all those visual images, are snagging on the filament, one by one. They twitch for a while, then they settle, and I'm able to look at them, manipulate them into the order of my life and study all the people and places and events and objects and feelings, slowly and carefully. I think I know my mother's face better now. Mad, isn't it?

But there's something else. Something's there that hasn't happened to me. It's perfectly clear. Bright. Golden.

It moves. Not in any hazy way – some of my memories are like through a doorscreen on some farmhouse in the Midwest – but alive, real. I really believe it's real. And I come across it anywhere in my chronology, it's as if it's the most important event of my life and it's happened over and over and over again, and yet I've never been there, never seen it, never lived it.

Someone's trespassed inside my head. And I don't know what it means.

It's on a hillside. The earth's caramel coloured and the vegetation's dry, like patchy scrub. We're near the top of the hill, but higher ones roll away into the distance behind. Their slopes are covered in clumps of olive trees. I've never seen an olive tree, though: I just know that's what they are.

It's mid morning: the shadows are long enough to tell me that. It's cool – or, at least, I don't see any heat haze – and there's a sense of ease, of affluence. It's not a hard place.

There's a man standing on the hillside. He's tall, over six feet. He's African, middle aged, and he looks wise. His hair's short. He's wearing a white t-shirt, khaki trousers and army boots, but there's no feeling of danger, he's not a threat: he's carrying a book in his hand, really carefully, like it's the most valuable thing in the world. I think if I look hard enough, I'll eventually be able to read the title on the spine. It's slim. Maybe poetry. He's relaxed and his midriff spills over his belt – just slightly, not enough to suggest he's lazy. It sounds daft, but I feel he's ... a wonder. I don't know why.

He's smiling at a child. A wee girl, about three. She's white-skinned and dark-haired, and wears a blue velvet dress, lace collar and hem. She's holding a yellow boat, made of wood, with a crisp white sail and a red rudder. The deck's polished and varnished. Her shoes are red. She doesn't wear socks: I think she forgot to put them on this morning.

The man bends down to her: his knees are like these fascinating, fluid levers lowering his body to her level. His movement's easy, constant. He puts the book on his knees and holds the child's shoulders gently. She smiles at him, but she doesn't know him: there's a look of surprise on her face. His t-shirt has a pocket over his left breast. He reaches into it with his right hand and takes out something small, really tiny, and holds it out to her, his hand covering it.

She looks at him and he nods. He makes a loose fist in front of her and her hands reach out: they look like cabbage-white butterflies they flutter so much. One by one, her fingers peel back his: they're playing a game, a silent game. His hand opens like a flower. There's no sound – none – but I'm sure she gasps. He's holding a nut. A small, brown nut. It's polished, cherrywood brown, smooth. She traces a finger over it, lightly: she's afraid it'll jump or vanish. Then she lifts it, holds it tightly against her chest.

That's all. That's what's been left in my head. And it makes me feel ... soothed. It's funny, I don't resent the intrusion.

I only know that it's been left there, by whatever happened that night. It isn't a forgotten memory resurfacing. It isn't a hallucination. It isn't imagination. It's real. I swear.

'Course, I made a mistake. Telling people. Folk've been phoning me all hours, priests and ministers and culty dafties. They think I've seen God: they get all excited when I tell them I heard a trumpet. Then I tell them the images I've got and it doesn't quite fit their thoughts on the matter: not really like angels, are they?

Why should what they're looking for be deposited in my head?

Anyway. I'm dead tired now. Would you mind going?

Okay?

III. Route Map

2 June

Dear Angela,

I don't quite know how to start this. The last time I saw you, I said I wouldn't phone you, but I never meant that. I really didn't. I always thought I'd be in touch again, and soon. It just never worked out like that, so I don't suppose you want to hear from me now. But I have to tell you some things that've happened to me.

I'm writing this in the car. I'm sitting in it at the edge of some cliffs down near Portpatrick. Well, I'm not right at the edge. I'm not planning suicide or anything! (Would you care? – I hope so). I'm just sitting here, maybe fifty feet away from the edge, and I brought myself here. Just brought myself here. Set off at six this morning (now it's early afternoon) and I knew where I wanted to go and what it would look like when I got here, but I didn't plan it or anything like that. I just set off and took the right road and the right turns – and here I am.

It's been happening a lot since I last saw you. Do you remember? Course you do. I suppose I mean does it matter to you? Now. I don't know if you heard about the accident. With the taxi. I tried to hail a taxi after I left you, but it crashed. It was in the papers for a while, because some weird things happened after it: a jazz musician that battered his lodger because of it, the blind guy they said'd seen an angel. I don't remember much about it – just a bright light and the brakes squealing. I woke up in hospital. They said I was wandering down the middle of the road, in shock, but I had burns too. Over my forehead and on my face and hands. Not bad, but they wept pus for a while. The driver had them too, apparently. The papers paid more attention to him because he used to be a footballer. Played for Scotland in the seventies. The doctors kept me in for tests (some guy in a tank top came from the university with a Geiger

Counter, for fuck's sake!). Jacqueline came to see me first. I think she was pleased that I was stuck in bed, she knew where I was. Not much chance of me gallivanting around with you, I suppose.

She was good to me. She never said anything about where I'd been that night – she must've known it was with you – just hugged me and said she was glad I was all right, and told me how the kids were doing. Stewart had been suspended from school again, I remember it. Told a teacher she was talking pants. He didn't want to come in to see me in case I gave him into trouble. Nicola threw her apple dessert at the kitchen wall, managed to break the clock. (She had a bowler's arm at 10 months old!) And that's what she did. Just talked about the family, as if nothing had happened between us, as if everything was normal.

So I stayed in for a week, but it was really odd when I got out. Jacqueline couldn't pick me up, she was working, so I said I'd get home myself. And I did. I went to the bus stop and I knew which bus to get, and which stop to get off at, and which bus to take next ... it was weird. I knew where I was going. Just instinctively knew.

I wanted to phone you then, but the burns were still scabby, still weeping a bit, and I had to change the bandages every day. It wasn't sore, just a bit ugly. I thought it'd scare you. And after that – it just always seemed to be that I'd phone you tomorrow. And then tomorrow. And then you realize you can't ever phone again.

What can I tell you? You said all sorts of things.

That I was just after sex, that I didn't respect you, that I should never have come near you because I knew there wasn't any future. All that stuff. And I agreed because I thought it was what you wanted to hear, what you needed to hear to move on. And maybe you were right. Because I couldn't deal with it then, I couldn't make the decision. How do you choose? I didn't know how to. It felt like the two halves of my brain were going to fucking kill each other, that there was a big shiny blade cutting between them, cutting through all the grey matter and it was spurting blood and brain fluid, and I couldn't think. Do you know, that morning, before I came to see you, I went into the cupboard for some cereal. Muesli. There was this packet of dried apricots, two or three left. I thought, I'll have them. I reached in for the packet, then pulled my hand away, then went back in. I must have done it eight or nine times, in and out, because I just couldn't decide. About apricots, for fuck's sake. I was in a mess. And you needed me to make a decision. I'm sorry.

Funny thing is, I still haven't.

But this thing, this directions thing, it's strange. Jacqueline's brother, Davie, the one that thinks I'm a shite, he came over a couple of weeks after I got out. He was taking his kids to Laser Quest, but he wanted to go to the big new shopping centre outside Renfrew before he went up to Glasgow, and he asked us the quickest way. Jacqueline didn't know, she said the motorway, but then I told him. I told him when to turn right, then left, which roundabout exit to take, what his mileage would be, even told him where there was a really bad pothole in the road. And then it got really weird, because I started telling him how to get from the shopping centre to Laser Quest, not just the centre of the town, but the nearest multi-storey car park, even to the space he should go to. Take the left fork out of the shopping centre, second exit at the roundabout, travel down three-quarters of a mile, take the third on the left by the Imo car wash ... he had to stop me, put his hands on my shoulders and tell me I was telling him too much. But I saw it. Like I was a homing pigeon, or like I had some sort of global positioning system in my head.

You probably don't want to hear about it. You probably don't want to hear about anything from me. There you go. I know you'll never trust me, but I didn't mean to let you down. I just kept giving in to the voice shouting loudest, the voice nearest, most immediate. I'd say anything, and really really mean it at the time, and then another voice would shout, and I'd say, 'Okay, okay, I'll do that.' I'm not proud of myself, I'm not trying to justify myself, honestly. I was a bastard, to you and to Jacqueline. But I'd been so unhappy, and you gave me the trembling knees and the pounding heart and the sledgehammer in the gut I haven't felt for fifteen years. You could have gone back to the temp agency any time, and I'd never have seen you again, and I just couldn't miss out on you.

I remember the first time you came to the station. I was reading out traffic announcements on air and you walked by the booth window. Long red hair and green eyes: it was like you had a bar code on you. I lost it in mid-sentence, had to read the same broken-down lorry on the A77 four times. You walked in this pocket of fresh air that set my head reeling. Do you remember the first time we came together? I hardly remember the sex – just that it was good – but right after it hit us like a train, you turned your head away and smiled and closed your eyes and pulled the sheet up over your face because you were so shy, so embarrassed at letting go. But do you know the best? We went shopping and you'd bought some Spanish onions and I helped you unpack and I found that cream and pale blue bowl in your cupboard. I piled the purple onions in it and I held it up to you and said it looked really pretty and you gave me that secret smile you used to have and came over and kissed me so hard. You said you'd never forget me doing that or saying that. I've never loved anyone more than I loved you at that moment.

And I had to leave you aside, and I'm thirty-six and I don't know if I'll ever feel that again. That scares me. Serves me right.

After the burns cleared up on my hands, I could drive again, and I couldn't get enough. I'd get in the car and just drive. And every time I'd stop, I'd know I'd got just where I should be. And it's not always like here, this is nice. It's a lovely view. The sea's steely grey and the sun's glinting off the waves and there's a wee yellow yacht scudding across the water. But sometimes, it's down all sorts of back streets to look at the rear wall of a factory, or over a wee rutted track that's got a pile of peats at the end of it. One time I turned up to look at a big tenement, and there was a pair of yellow curtains that reminded me of yours. Then there was a three-hour drive to the far end of a supermarket car park, and I sat looking at some playing fields through this chain-link fence at a game of football between some pub sides. One team had red stripes, the other had blue hoops. The noise, the shouting and cheering, the swearing, and these stripes and hoops really vivid, running about – it just felt perfect. Perfect.

Jacqueline worries about it, about me. She never seems to question where I've been, just looks concerned. She thinks I'm having a breakdown, she's told the kids not to bother their dad. She talked me into seeing the doctor, who talked me into seeing a psychotherapist: it's quite good. Apparently, lots of men of my age have a problem with who they are, with their place in life. So talking about it's been okay.

But I can't get it through to them that it all seems so normal to me, that I just think it and go. When I realized how it works, I almost fainted at the thought of it, the enormity of it.

You see, every single road in this country is connected to every single other road in the country. Every place to every place. There aren't any blind alleys, no roads to nowhere, no wrong turns. You can drive from a wee cul-de-sac in Cornwall to a farm outside Wick because it's all joined up, all part of the same huge network that gets us from A to B with any letters you like in between. Think about it: <u>everything's</u> connected. That means you can get to wherever you want from wherever you are. It's so easy. And sometimes the straightness of the *road you have to take to get from one place to another is incredible, so simple you wouldn't believe it. I drove to a wheatfield in Hertfordshire, sat there admiring a wee clump of trees in the middle of it, and do you know how many turns I made? All in all? Fourteen. That's all. Fourteen turns and I was on another planet.*

It's getting a bit grey. Looks like a storm might be blowing in, there's lots of black clouds on the horizon, and the wind's picking up. There's a few bits of litter swirling around the car – plastic bags and bits of newspaper and stuff: a picture of some politician's just stuck itself to the windscreen.

It's getting a bit cold, so I've put the engine on. I know I'm never going to see you again, but I can't help wishing you were here for a cuddle. I get such strange impulses these days – writing this letter's one of them I suppose. I've got the hazard lights on. The rhythm's quite soothing. They're ticking away, front and back, left and right.

Fuck knows where I'll end up going next. Maybe I'll send you a postcard.

Then again, maybe not.

Paul

XXX

The Wolfclaw Chronicles
Tom Bryan
A powerful debut novel bridging the cultures of Ireland, Russia, Canada, Scotland and England.
ISBN 1-903238-10-2
Price £9.99

Rousseau Moon
David Cameron
Lyrical, intense, sensitive, foreboding – a remarkable first collection.
ISBN 1-903238-15-3
Price £9.99

Life Drawing
Linda Cracknell
The eagerly awaited first collection from an award-winning writer.
ISBN 1-903238-13-7
Price £9.99

Hi Bonnybrig & Other Greetings
Shug Hanlan
Strikingly original short stories and a very funny novella.
ISBN 1-903238-16-1
Price £9.99

The Tin Man
Martin Shannon
A debut novel from a new and exciting young writer.
ISBN 1-903238-11-0
Price £9.99

Occasional Demons
Raymond Soltysek
A dark, menacing and quite dazzling collection from one of Scotland's most talented new writers.
ISBN 1-903238-12-9
Price £9.99

About 11:9

Who makes the decisions?

Our aims

Supported by the Scottish Arts Council National Lottery Fund and partnership funding, 11:9 publish the work of writers both unknown and established, living and working in Scotland or from a Scottish background.
11:9's brief is to publish contemporary literary novels, and is actively searching for new talent. If you wish to submit work send an introductory letter, a brief synopsis of your novel, a biographical note about yourself and two typed sample chapters to: Editorial Administrator, 11:9, Neil Wilson Publishing Ltd, Suite 303a, The Pentagon Centre, 36 Washington Street, Glasgow, G3 8AZ. Details are also available from our website at **www.11-9.co.uk.**

If you would like to be added to a mailing list about future publications, either register on our website or send your name and address to 11:9, Neil Wilson Publishing Ltd, Suite 303a, The Pentagon Centre, 36 Washington Street, Glasgow, G3 8AZ.

11:9 refers to 11 September 1997 when the Scottish people voted to re-establish their parliament in Edinburgh